I0622260

Summer Feet

BETSY ROBERTS

First Published 2015

Published by Malua Publishing, Australia

Copyright © Betsy Roberts 2015

All rights reserved. Without limiting the rights under copyright reserved above, no part of this publication may be reproduced, stored in or introduced into a retrieval system, or transmitted, in any form or by any means (electronic, mechanical, photo-copying, recording or otherwise) without the prior written permission of both the author and the publisher of this book, except where permitted by law.

ISBN 978 0 9946296 0 9

Design and production by Chris Roberts

Photographs © Chris Roberts and © Roberts family

Permission to reproduce quotes from original family letters to home written during WW2 given by Dick Roberts.

For Mum and Dad & the Jacarandas,

Always with us, but now sadly, part of our past.

Prologue

TURN AROUND, TURN around and face the sea, for only the sea remains. They have cut back the mulberry tree – there is no one now to eat the fruit. The jacaranda flowers still bloom and fall, but more quietly it seems, and the old trees creak and bend lower with the winds of autumn. The house is there still, but not as it was. The pictures fade: drowned in sea spray, in falling leaves …

But we are grown now; we know the words to tell of these things gone: mud pies in the fuel stove, ladybirds in the lemon tree, Christmas beetles like iridescent aeroplanes, pencil marks on the kitchen door: the measurement of ages, of growing; treading barefoot through the years.

It's the summers I remember, warm days we felt with our feet. School shoes were the heralds of doom, unearthed and polished at the end of summer. Stiff black lace-ups, never the strappy patent leathers that might have compensated; there lay the path to permed hair and pierced ears. Feet were scrubbed clean, finally, of their various fruit and vegetable colours, cased in cotton fresh white socks and tied into the shoes.

Summers at the beach, stepping lightly over wet packed sand, trying to leave the perfect footprint, or walking on our heels: the amazing puzzle of the legless man. Stabbing our feet across fields of hot, soft sand to make the grains shriek like ripping silk. Each day we wanted to be first, so ours might be the best fresh trail of prints on the morning beach; and each day, by dusk, the beach was another relief map; a moonscape pitted by a million nameless feet. And where sea met land, along the line of coffee froth, the sodden sand had reformed, dark and smooth.

Hours in the water, from the first icy toe-dip to the shrivelled amphibious white of feet too long immersed. Treading on water. Treading on the seabed; shocked sometimes by something unseen, something slimy: seaweed, jellyfish, who knew what; and suddenly the sea was not your friend. Twisting down in the quicksand at tideline, getting smaller and shorter, calf-deep, till the smooth, cold curve of a buried pipi shell rewarded probing toes.

Days in the yard, which, by November had turned lavender, then brown; lazy days, squelching through a soft mulch quilt of fallen flowers, we lay beneath the jacarandas and under the hose, watching rainbows in the spray through fanned fingers and toes. Then came the mulberries – jams, pies, bucket-loads of berries and cream; purple lipstick, purple feet, and perfect purple footprints for detective games on the concrete path. Later on the mangoes fell, overripe from laden trees; far too many to be eaten. Golden and bursting with sticky juice in the wet heat of late summer, then black and pulpy underfoot; better than banana skins.

And everywhere, the red clay soil: terracotta talc. Soft and powdery in the dry, it settled in and traced the lines of elbows, knees and toes. And after rain, in the gully road, we slipped and slid on the smooth, wet mud; the slick red mud that wormed through toes like Vegemite through Sao holes, like oil paint from tubes.

Everything grew in that soil. The cracks in the concrete path flourished with splashes of impatiens and dark, spongy, cushions of moss. I grew – and having grown, like many a country child, was transplanted to the city to live and learn.

I remember winters.

I remember my first sad view, waking on the bus: the mute struggle of three cold and naked trees, poking through a square in Anzac Place. And in those first three leafless years, I gleaned amusement only from learning how to catch the city trains and buses, and ride them with the city face of wise and bored detachment.

I also learned that one does not walk barefoot on city footpaths. Those stained, free feet of childhood could not thus be reclaimed.

But I could wear patent leather if I wanted to.

Part One

Leaving

"Tomorrow to fresh woods, and pastures new."

John Milton 'Lycidas'

Shell Bay, June 1952

MARGARET

SHE'D SMOKED SO many cigarettes that she felt nauseous. Even the soothing rhythms of knit-one-purl-one had to be put aside; hands slippery on the needles, too many dropped stitches. She closed her eyes against the too-familiar, too-small space she could never call home. The push-button cupboards that flew open every time the Ute hit a bump, the sink that wasn't wide enough to fit a dinner plate, the makeshift bunks that never looked tidy or properly anchored.

They'd arrived at Shell Bay Camping Ground on Saturday. Then the rain came. Nearly three days of leaden skies and heavy, soaking rain, compacting the grey sand around them and drumming on the roof. The awning bowed under a weight of water that sluiced over the scalloped edge at regular intervals in a glittering curtain and carved a moat around the caravan.

She'd begged him to leave the annex up. At least that way they could keep the north windows open and the van wouldn't smell so much like wet dressing sheds. Something else with which she'd become too well acquainted recently.

Most of the campers had left – it was already early June – although the locals spent a lot of time ruminating over what was apparently freakish North Coast weather. But Rob, ever inquisitive, had found that even mild interest in the elements was rewarded with dark and lengthy tales of farms sliding down hills, livestock being blown away. Which she'd rather he hadn't relayed to her.

The family had been travelling for two months.

They were all restless, but for different reasons. She knew Rob was ready to move on. He wasn't really sold on the idea of banana farming; already dreaming of pastures farther north. The rain had been so relentless there'd hardly been a chance to look around anyway. The girls were just sick of being cooped up. They'd been pretty good, but how many games of I Spy could you play before there was no more to spy in a small caravan.

Margaret would simply have been much happier in their safe and comfortable house in Melbourne. But it no longer was theirs; occupied now by Rob's presumably satisfied successor in the world of advertising. And while rain was rain – god knows they'd had enough of that down there – this was different.

And she'd heard the whispers of worse to come, the current lull a false reprieve she knew, simply a time for the weather to retreat and gather strength. She also knew her terrors were irrational. The chances of being struck by lightning were slight. But no amount of reason could quell the vertigo, the creeping paralysis. It came with the first sense of an impending storm, and grew with the darkening of the weather.

The fear was in the waiting.

The change in the air had crept in quietly, but their awareness that the steady drip and beat on the roof had ceased was quite sudden. At mid-afternoon on Monday, they looked out to a world that had the weird, silent clarity of a surrealist painting. There was no movement. There were no tents left on the headland; just the pines, black arrowheads ranged along the horizon and backlit by a steely yellow sky. The silence was broken only by the bark of a distant dog. A short, anxious yelp that slid into a mournful howl.

A child's swimsuit, a tiny, spotted, bubble costume, forgotten, sagged alone on the clothesline behind the amenities block.

The girls had leapt out into the strange, watching landscape, rushing about the park with all the exuberance of liberated animals and tumbling down the dunes to investigate the beach. Rob had gone to pick up some basic groceries and check the forecast.

Margaret stayed in the van. Things to do: separate wet towels from damp ones, check what clothes were still clean and dry, prepare vegetables for an early tea – but even folding towels took an effort of will.

She knew they were the only occupied van left in the park. Those crazy people from Melbourne, who swim in the middle of winter, spend all day fishing and never catch anything. (If they'd been everywhere a week earlier, apparently, they'd have been able to lift the fish out with their hands). It had become a competition between the girls to see who could be first to spot the local seafood shop each time they settled to camp for a few days. 'We know where all the fish are, Dad.'

No fish and chips tonight. The shop had closed early.

The sky was darkening with rolling banks of cloud that looked as though they were being inflated by the occasional rumblings sounding on the horizon; reverberations, still distant enough that they might have been trucks on the highway, or even a goods train behind the headland.

Rob came back. 'I'm going to put the annex down, love,' he said, 'before it gets dark.'

She was finding it difficult to breathe.

The girls burst in, Cathy eager with important facts …

'That's stupid,' Susan was saying. 'Birds don't know anything.'

'John at the fish shop told me,' said Cathy. 'He said you'd better go in pet. All the birds have gone home. They know.'

'Mum, Cathy's being dumb. How would the birds know?' …

'Know what?' said Margaret. But she didn't want to know. If you didn't talk about it, it might not happen.

'About storms - really big ones. John says he always knows when there's one coming because of the storm birds.'

'Rob ...?' He'd been talking to John too, and to Norm and Elsie from the Kiosk. She'd heard them sloshing around the park, putting away bins, beach chairs and benches that weren't concreted down. Words and phrases had floated, unwelcome, into her consciousness, *bit of a blow on the way ... batten down the hatches ... prevailing winds ... depressions ... low moving down the coast ...* and Rob's voice, barely controlled excitement as he recalled similar experiences from his time in Fiji, before the war.

He'd tightened the tarp and was checking the window screens. 'It's all right love,' he said now. 'There's a storm on the way, but we'll be okay. Norm says we're in the best spot here anyway, in the lee of the headland. Protected by the dunes too. Just need to make sure we put the hatch down and shut the windows. If the van was going to leak we'd have been bailing out water days ago.'

About half past four, the air along the dunes started to move. A barely perceptible shiver ran through the casuarinas, and the spot-ted swimsuit, missed by Elsie, lifted, ballooned briefly, and flopped. Margaret wanted to rescue it, but she knew she could not walk out into that hostile twilight.

'We're having tea early tonight girls. Just have a wash down in the sink – I don't want you to go out again now,' steadying her own hands with the patting dry of sandy feet, the brushing out of tangled hair.

It was almost dark in the van. She wasted three matches before she got the lantern going. Every time she smelt the kero and watched the wick take up the blue flame, she imagined them all being burned in their beds. Trapped in a plywood eggshell.

At least you could put out the lamp. Turn off the primus. You couldn't stop the wind. You didn't know where to stand to avoid a shaft of lightning.

She'd been about the same age Susan was now, washing up while her cousin dried. Standing at the kitchen window when the rifle shot that was a clap of thunder shook the whole house. One of those freak electrical storms of the Sydney summer. Everything had gone black and white and the tree where their cubby was, the tree they'd been climbing that afternoon, split in half and turned into a torch before their eyes. Then just black. A terrible darkness. And until the rest of the family came running and screaming into the kitchen, she thought she'd died.

'We'll be right love,' Rob said again. 'Be all over by the morning.'

When it comes, the wind begins as a distant keening siren, gathering pitch and strength as it howls over the headland in continuous waves. It strips the pines, snaps pandanus palms, and funnels into the bay, gusting and fluctuating in vicious, chaotic squalls, and it carries back the rain – relentless, horizontal sheets that flash through the roaring black night.

Margaret, close to tears, curls into a stiff cocoon, waiting for the spearing branch that is going to split the roof, the screaming blast that will hurl them into oblivion. As each fresh crack of thunder explodes in the electric air she feels her body convulse.

The van rocks, protected from the fiercest power of the gale, but buffeted by the driving rain and the constant attack and retreat of the swirling winds. The primus rattles on the bench, and an enamel plate clatters onto the lino, but the only real casualty is a wire screen that is torn from one of the east-facing windows and spins northward across the park.

Rob and the girls play guessing games in the dark, till Cathy and Susan, over-excited by the wild weather, finally drift off to sleep. He holds Margaret close in their narrow bunk, and talks of the future. How it will all be worth it when they find the right piece of land. He'll be his own boss. They'll work together. Living near the beach. No more freezing winters.

She tries to count something other than the beats between explosions of thunder and flashes of lightning. She doesn't have the strength to put into words how she feels about living near the beach just now. She can feel his energy, but it doesn't stop the despair. Each jolt of the van sends waves of fear through her. She has named every character in *Oliver Twist*, listed the casts of Shakespeare's comedies, and started on the histories, till eventually she manages fitful catnaps just before dawn.

The van is still.

The howling whine of the wind died as suddenly as it began, now only an echo in the memory. A group of butcherbirds test their scales in the clear air, rippling above the solid boom of the brown ocean, a steady beat for the new day.

Rob's up and about, 'Well that's all over. We've weathered the worst of it. A couple of days here till the car's right, then we can get on.'

Margaret lies facing the wall, drained and tired. No it isn't, she thinks. It isn't all over. We're only half way there, wherever there is.

Outside, a fluffy ridge of foam lines the dunes. From time to time, little soapy clouds break off and blow gently down to the park, over rivers of sand, palm leaves and pine needles. Most of the casuarinas are still standing, draped with strange offerings from the sea. A scrap of spotted material lies almost buried in the debris, its strap still knotted to the dangling remains of the Shell Bay Park washing line.

Shell Bay, 1952

CATHY

WE WENT TO Coolac first. Well after all the tea chests and suitcases were packed up and the new car. The tea chests didn't have tea in them but that's what they call them because explorers and people used to take them on ships to carry tea leaves back from other countries for the queen Susan said. I think Dad told her that but anyway they had all things like our cups and saucers and books and plates and cold clothes packed in them because there wouldn't be enough room even though it was a new car and it was a utility so it could pull the caravan and we'd all have to sit in the front. We had to find a place to call home first and it should be warm where we were going so we would only need swimmers and things. The men who came and packed did it all pretty fast even with wrapping all our things in torn up newspaper so they wouldn't break. A sterling job Dad called it.

So after all that and after Mum sorting things and cleaning for donkeys years the new caravan we would be sleeping in got packed too and then we went to Coolac. To say goodbye to Aunty Belle and Uncle John and our cousins Tim and Lucy because we were heading for greener pastures. It would be good to stay there all the time because they have horses Lucy and Susan could ride a lot as long as they didn't go fast and I think Tim and me could get married when we grow up but Susan says we're cousins and you can't. The only thing Susan really truly wants is a horse or maybe a pony and she said to Dad this looks like green pasture but Mum said it probably wasn't green enough. It was Susan's birthday while we were at

Aunty Belle's place and she didn't get a horse for a present but Aunty Belle made a lovely cake. Chocolate icing with ten candles.

Susan didn't want to go away from Melbourne because she won't be able to see her friends anymore but Mum said she can write letters every week and Dad said on our journey we can pretend to be explorers just like she was learning about at school and she could teach me because we would see lots of geography and nature study. She likes to tell me things because so far I only go to pre-school but sometimes she is a bossy teacher. Mum said when we get to where we are going we will go to a new school.

Anyway Dad wants to maybe have our own farm so we're driving for a long time away from the city but not years and years till we find a good one. Susan said a ranch would be good and Dad said it won't be that sort of farm but if everyone is really good we might get a horse one day. We drove over the mountains after Coolac and up the highest mountain in Australia. I never saw snow before and it was very cold and wet but fun to play in. Then we stopped in Sydney at Grandma's to say goodbye and see all those aunties and uncles that were Mum's brothers and sisters when she was little and Mum got pretty sad.

There was a nice place with the beach at Forster and Dad nearly decided we would have a motel to own but it was good that he didn't because the man said motels are just be a flash in the pan and the next place we stayed was Shell Bay and that was an exciting adventure. On the way it was awful because the new car couldn't get up the steep hill just before Shell Bay with us all still in the car and all the suitcases and the caravan to pull. We had to get out and walk up the hill and take some suitcases out of the caravan so it wasn't too heavy or the car would give up the ghost and blow a gasket. So it didn't but it was nearly dark by the time we got settled down in the caravan park because then Dad had to walk all the way back to the bottom of the hill and carry the suitcases back from where Mum and us were waiting and everyone got really hot and tired and cranky. Then when we woke up to go for a swim it looked like rain. But we could see way way out from where the lighthouse was and there were grey waves with white tops all over the water. They call that White Horses Dad said and they come when it's windy on the sea.

There were no real horses but lots of bananas and the car had to be fixed and there was lots of rain and we even had a cyclone, but on the day after the big storm we had lunch at the Railway Station and the man showed us around the platform and how the signals worked. It was good when the rain stopped too because Susan always wins at I Spy and Snap unless she lets me win on purpose and that's silly and the rain was so hard you couldn't hear the wireless and when the storm was on we had to have tea before it got dark. And we had to go straight to bed because it might be dangerous if we had to light the lamp and Susan was cranky because she was nearly finished *My Friend Flicka* that she got for her birthday. Mum said you did finish it and she said I'm reading the good bits again.

But everything was terrific after the storm.

Me and Susan went out with Dad early in the morning after it finished to Inspect the Damage and to let Mum catch up on a bit of sleep. Dad said the sea would be very rough and we still had to watch our steps but it was low tide so there would be lots of interesting things washed up called debris. We helped Norm and Elsie pick up all the bits of tree and everything that was lying around the park and Norm said that debris came right up over the dunes. That's how strong the wind was. All the she oaks looked like soggy Christmas trees with seaweed and bits of newspaper and shells instead of bells and tinsel. And the froth was funny. This big fluffy browny blanket all over the sandhills. We had our swimmers on so

10

Dad let us roll down to the beach and we ended up with sort of brown and white froth coats on.

There were huge lumps of seaweed and crab claws and dead fish everywhere that smelled horrible and you never saw such big loud waves. Dad said we couldn't swim because there would be dumpers and the rip would take us out to sea in no time. I couldn't see any torn water but that's why rips are so dangerous. You have to be careful. The water was all weedy and browny grey anyway and pretty scary and where the river came out to the sea from the side of the park the water looked like tea out of the teapot the way Grandma likes it but we paddled in it and washed off the foam and it made our hair feel really soft.

You could hardly see any sand for all the debris and white smooth branches that Dad said were called driftwood and might have come from a long way away maybe even another country. I said maybe Melbourne and Susan said Melbourne's not another country and Dad said well the storm did come up from the south so I said see Smartypants maybe it's from Rosebud. But she still said she bets it was Spain or Tahiti.

Anyway we walked along the beach a bit to see if there were any good driftwoods Dad could make something nice with or we could just save but it was better to see if maybe there was a good shell for an ashtray for Mum because there wasn't that much room for branches in the caravan. We found lots of pretty bits of blue and green glass but they were a bit sharp sometimes and there weren't many whole shells because the waves had been crashing down so hard. Then Susan said can you keep a secret cross your heart and hope to die she said and I said yes and she said she found a seahorse hidden under some seaweed and she made a wish that meant she would get a horse when we find the farm and then she put it back in the sea she said. So it wasn't there now. Well I won't tell but I think it's a fib and anyway we did find one nice almost whole shell for Mum.

In the afternoon we went up the headland for a walk and even some of the really big old pine trees were broken and tipping over and we still nearly got blown away if we weren't careful.

Anyway the car is fixed again now and it's my turn to have the window seat on Mum's lap. Dad still doesn't know when we'll live in a house instead of a caravan but he says when we get there it will be nice and sunny all the time and we'll be able to swim and see places Captain Cook discovered. Mum didn't say anything but Susan said I hope it won't be too warm for horses and punched my leg but not really hard.

Shell Bay, June 1952

MARGARET

SHE STARES DULLY over her husband's shoulder at the watery ruins of the caravan park.

'I'd better go and get the Chev sorted out, love,' he says. 'Bring the kids up later for a spot of lunch and I'll meet you. Garage is just behind the shunting yards there – round the Headland. Trains are still running so the Station café'll be open. It looked all right.'

She shepherds the girls towards a corner table, glances down to make sure it's been wiped since the last peas and gravy, and sinks wearily onto the bench.

Fly-spotted ceiling fans, dusty lace curtains; wood panelling, cool and dark. Glass shelves behind the counter with Old Gold chocolate boxes, faded, milkshake glasses upside down and Minties; pinafored waitress on guard. The Railway Refreshment Rooms – they could be back in Main Street Benalla, Goulburn or Gosford. Except then, Lunch at The Café still seemed like a treat to her, as well as the kids. She fishes a book out of her bag and lines up the ashtray with her cigarettes and matches. Sets up a little fortress with the honey pot – a squat blue ceramic beehive still there from break-fast – the salt and peppershakers, the Holbrook's bottle, and a surprising addition.

'Look Mum, a plate of mothballs.'

'No, they're not mothballs sweetie.'

'What a dumbo,' Susan rolls her eyes with all the world-weariness of one older and wiser by six years, but her attention is already caught by photographs on the far wall. She slides back out to make a closer inspection.

'Mothballs,' insists Cathy.

'They're mints, lollies – here,' Margaret passes one across the table, and pops one into her own mouth.

And remembers the smell, not of mints, but of mothballs. Tea chests and mothballs. The smells that surrounded the beginnings of this journey, already months old, its ending a blank horizon. Sorting out drawers and cupboards – what to take and what to leave. Heavy coats, fusty from summer storage, relegated again to the dark, along with most of their possessions, to the chests that will follow when there is somewhere to unpack them.

A sudden mental image of herself and Rob, struggling across some godforsaken Burke and Wills landscape towards a mirage labelled 'The Far North', almost makes her smile. It isn't funny. She drags her mind back to the present. There are posters on the walls – *Take the Train – Take a Kodak*, and the photographs that caught Susan's eye, sepia views of favoured destinations: The Three Sisters, Jenolan Caves. What Margaret's been staring at above their own table is a framed map of New South Wales, rail lines marked in red.

The waitress appears and slips a plastic covered menu onto the table. 'Thanks,' says Margaret, still mesmerized by that red line, southbound, rounded letters spelling out Taree, Maitland, Gosford, Sydney, … 'Susan, come and sit down – you can have a look after lunch …' and to the waitress's caustic 'You want me to come back later?'

'Sorry - just some sandwiches please. A mixed plate, and a round of plain tomato.'

'Marto sand witches!' Cathy pipes up excitedly.

'Compost. Mum, what's fruit compost?' Susan has been reading aloud through the menu, offering Cathy various tempting alternatives she knows they won't be allowed to have.

14

'Compote,' says Margaret, 'it's French – mixed fruit. That's the breakfast menu. If you behave we'll see about an ice-cream later.'

'Sandwiches,' says Susan gloomily, and wanders off again.

'Two glasses of milk too, please. I'll have a pot of tea after,' Margaret finally glances up at the waitress, who has been all but tapping her foot, and has now turned to an older woman struggling through the door behind a crocheted travel rug and numerous bulging string bags.

'Mrs. Timmins - how are you? Off to the big smoke now, eh?'

'I'm not too bad love, thanks. It's Dot, isn't it? Yes, back to the city after all these years. You know – it's been hard, but it'll be nice to be with the family. Yes, tea thanks dear. Came in a bit early to book the luggage through,' she says, shrugging off a rusty black travel coat – *Oh please*, thinks Margaret, *don't sit there* ... 'You don't mind if I park myself here do you love?' ... *well to be quite honest* ...'save Dot setting another table. You look like you could do with a bit of company.'

She settles her bulk next to the suddenly shy toddler, rearranging stray wisps of gray hair and hatpins. 'Hullo, little one. That's a lovely jumper. Did your Mummy make that?'

'Wuff, Snuff 'n Tuff,' says Cathy, proudly puffing out her chest to display the three little dogs ... *just like Bondi or Rosebud – spread out the towels, and suddenly it's the most popular spot on the beach* ... Margaret edges closer to the corner and eyes her book sadly.

'Do a bit of knitting myself – for the grand kiddies mainly – now Noel's gone' ... *not the ' life hasn't been the same without Noel' story – not now* ... I'm Evelyn by the way,' Mrs. Timmins turns back to Margaret, 'Evelyn Timmins.'

'Margaret Williams,' she smiles weakly, the familiar ache starting just behind her right eye.

Susan strolls over, regards the milk and sandwiches sulkily, then bestows her sparkling Ipana smile for strangers on Mrs. Timmins,

15

'Hullo, we live in a caravan. And everything got wet. Where do you live?'

'Susan, don't be rude. Mrs. Timmins is just having a cup of tea before she catches the train.'

'That's all right love … and look at your cardie. Fairisle too! What a clever Mummy.'

'Mum knits all our clothes. I was allowed to have my hair cut before we left home because plaits are a nuisance, but Cathy's still got plaits.'

'It's lovely hair too.'

Susan has the blue eyes and blond hair of Rob's first wife. Cathy owes her hazel eyes and fair skin to a fairly even mixture of what he jokingly refers to as Margaret's "bog Irish" and his own Orange ancestry. The contrast between the two is something Margaret sees no need to elucidate when people say, as Mrs. Timmins does now, 'They don't look at all alike, do they?'

'We're having sandwiches;' Susan continues brightly, 'Cathy still pretends she can't say tomato sandwiches properly, but she can really. I wanted compost but Mum says we only have that for breakfast.'

'Susan, for heavens' sake …'

Cathy starts giggling, 'Compost sand witches, mothball sand . .'

'Both of you – eat your sandwiches …'

'Fruit compost,' Susan explains, for the benefit of a slightly bemused Mrs. Timmins. 'It's French.'

'Ah, yes,' she smiles, 'you get that in hospitals too.' Margaret laughs in spite of herself, and Mrs. Timmins presses on: 'Not to be a sticky beak, but what's that you're reading?'

'*The Grapes of Wrath*,' says Margaret, 'I thought I'd read it again while we're travelling' … *get myself into the mood so to speak.*

'That's the one with Henry Fonda isn't it? Don't read a lot my-self, never had much time on the farm. Always get the Weekly though. It has some nice knitting patterns. Where are you headed?'

'I wish I knew,' Margaret smiles tightly and lights another ciga-rette, fingers curled – a habit as automatic now as once it was delib-erate – to hide freshly bitten fingernails.

She looks up as the waitress approaches with the teas. 'Could I get a Bex and a glass of water please?' and her eyes drift again towards the list of places they've left in their wake ... 'We left Mel-bourne in April ...' she pauses, the issue still too fresh and unre-solved to share with a stranger, but Mrs. Timmins is waiting expect-antly ... 'my husband wanted to get away from the rat race – be his own boss. Probably further up the coast somewhere.' She shrugs, 'Maybe farming.'

'And the car broke down, and Mum's scared of storms ...'

'Susan – look, if you've finished, you can take Cathy and have a look round the Station. Don't go off the platform, and don't be a nuisance to anyone.'

'Were you camped out in that last night? Dearie me – you'll be crossing Shell Bay off the list then I suppose. Generally June weath-er's beautiful here, but every so often we get a real lot of rain late April, May, then winter comes in with a couple of cyclones' ... *a couple of cyclones! Mother of god!* Margaret tries to block out the dreadful roar and crack of those dark hours ...

'It's been bad this year I must say. They say there'll be floods down Hunter way.'

'You're on a farm?'

'Was, love – near to thirty years. Started out in dairy. That's long days – up in the dark, out in the smelly bails in the middle of winter – got into bananas when we moved here. Good living in it nowa-days if you don't mind a bit of hard work – get back what you put in, my Noel always said.' She pauses, takes a sip of tea and continues when Margaret does not ask the obvious question. 'I lost Noel, not long back. Can't manage the place by myself, and our boys never wanted to stay on the farm. So we sold up. Going down to live with my daughter – she married a boy from Wollongong. That's where I come from - bout your age when I left too.'

'Thirty years,' says Margaret, her eyes straying again to the posters – *New South Wales Railway: Luxury Travel, Night & Day* ...

'Where's home for you love?'

'Sydney. Melbourne for the last couple of years. Rob – my husband, worked for an advertising firm.'

'City girl,' Mrs. Timmins nods. 'You get used to life in the country though. I hated it at first, but then I went down to visit the family, after the babies came – couldn't get back to the farm soon enough. You're working together a lot too – not like hubby going off all day to an office. That's one of the nice things. And some of the country's lovely. All the coast, from here up to the border. You're bound to find a nice place ... heavens, look at the time! I'd better be making tracks. It was nice to meet you love ... and listen,' she says, taking a dog-eared booklet out of her bag, 'you might want this. I won't be needing it anymore.'

She is alone at last with *The Grapes of Wrath*, but the hoped for quiet read and cup of tea are interrupted by the noisy and apparently late arrival of the afternoon waitress ...

'Sorry Dottie' ... 'That's ok Shirl, thought the valley road might've gone under' ... 'bails nearly blew over, not too much damage but ... water's gone down now. Wasn't that Mrs.Timmins?' ... 'Yeah, going down to live with Stu and Laurel' ...

Margaret shifts uncomfortably. Their voices carry in the otherwise empty café, and she feels like a spy. Damn Rob; how many times has she been alone in similar situations over these last months while he gets caught up in some exploration or other ...'For good?

What about their farm?' ... 'Had to sell ... there by herself. Too much for her with the bananas. But jeez, you couldn't stay, could you? Not after that. She found him, you know – pinned underneath the wheels he was ...'

Page forty-three of Margaret's book becomes a blur.

'I know ... I still get the horrors when I think about it. Only the other day I said to Charlie, you keep that up – roaring up and down those cow paddocks – you keep that up, I said, and you'll get yourself killed. Just like Noel Timmins. Bloody tractors ... what's she staring at? Bit longer and she might know us next time!'

Margaret's face burns as she looks away towards the door, angry now. What the hell can be taking him this long ...

'Dunno ...shh' ... whispered fragments still hiss across the room ... *'not from round here ... tickets on herself ... fancy slacks, sandals with all those straps ... something off a Fantales packet ... couple of kids, must've been a kid herself when she had the first one. Where's the husband ... been wolfing the Craven A's. Anyway, so poor Mrs. Timmins, she'd be mad to stay here. Reckon she deserves a rest, too ...'*

Her pause is punctuated by the creak and bang of the platform door ...

'Ah, here's the man in the picture, I'd say. Not bad either.'

'Think so? Looks a bit older than her, but could be.'

Margaret, head deliberately averted, knows by the changed tenor of the conversation, that Rob must have walked in – finally. The old charm, she thinks, the boyish grin, works with them all. Bosses' wives, nurses, waitresses ... he's not a tall man, but it's a stride rather than a walk. Randwick was where they met; and that's it – he's always put her in mind of a racehorse.

He throws a cheery 'Afternoon,' and half wave towards the women at the counter, 'not too late for some tucker I hope?' and eases into the seat opposite Margaret.

'Took a bit longer than I thought love – you had lunch? Got talking to the chap at the garage. He knows Booralla, believe it or not. Says there's lots of good land going up there … '

She slides her hand away from his and pushes the menu across the table. 'You'd better order if you want something to eat.'

'Where are the girls?'

'Just looking around. They can't be stuck inside all day.'

'Good'oh. Susan's probably got Cathy learning the street names off by heart. The Ute should be ready tomorrow, but we'll stay here a few days – get everything dried out. You still look a bit pale love. They say the rain's just about gone. Everything ship shape with the van?'

'Apart from looking like a Chinese laundry and being in the middle of a lake, wonderful.' She pours the last of the tea into her cup, scrapes some sugar, not enough, out of the bowl, 'there's never any sugar in these places!'

And suddenly there is Shirley, smiling at Rob, pencil poised, waiting to take his order.

'You weren't thinking of dairy were you?'

He all but springs to attention at this hint of renewed interest in their search for a better life. Early awareness of this power flattered and amazed her, but it sits more heavily now. She is fatigued somehow by the responsibility.

'*We* weren't thinking … no, don't fancy the early mornings. That's one of the things we're leaving behind. That, or at least the choice of getting up early or not. Thanks,' he smiles at Shirley, 'this looks beaut. Oh, and that sugar bowl's just about empty.'

'Right you are,' she whips a full one from a nearby table and swaps theirs with a flourish. He tips her a wink and offers Margaret the new sugar.

'Dairy,' he continues, 'no - small crops; should be warm enough. Bananas maybe, if we can get the right aspect, or beef cattle. We'll see. Apparently the soil's so good up there, plant anything it's a foot tall next week. And prices are sky high. For crops I mean. That's pretty much what Arthur told me too.'

' *"You can pick oranges right off the trees"* ', she murmurs, avoiding his gaze.

He glances at the paperback on the table, 'We're not the Joads. We weren't forced to do this love, and we're certainly not going to end up living in a box-car, picking cotton.'

Margaret lights a cigarette – *just remind me what the choices were, Rob* - she'll need another packet before they leave. She can still taste the tart analgesic powder, and the headache shows no signs of retreating. The discarded tomatoey crusts of Cathy's sandwich look like bleeding cuts on the plate, still not cleared when Rob's meal arrived. His egg yolks are spreading – almost raw steak in a yellow puddle – just the way he likes it. The faint imprint of someone else's lipstick still frames the little crown in the NSWGR logo on his teacup.

She fights down a wave of nausea and concentrates on the lengthening tip of her cigarette. *If I can smoke this without having to ash*, she thinks, *I'll get through this trip.*

'What about tractors?' The words are almost choked out.

'What do you mean?'

'Would we need one?'

'Well, I'd say so,' he grins, 'don't imagine messing around with draught horses. They're coming up with new attachments all the time too, new methods of ploughing.' He plunges on through the silence. 'We'd be getting a place sorted out first though darl, first things first. I mean there'll be clearing and planting to do – if we find somewhere, say, by August, September – so we can get a summer crop in. But if not, it isn't the end of the world. That's what this is all about – having the weather for a boss, instead of kowtowing to some no-hoper whose only talent is being the managing director's nephew …'

21

SUMMER FEET

The feathery column of ash that is now most of her cigarette sags and drops to the table. 'That could have been you in a year's time; the partnership – our sons could …'

'Yes – at a price I'm not prepared to pay …'

'Keep your voice down.'

'What? How many times did we talk about this? God, I thought you were happy to get out of Melbourne – the heat, the cold, the flies, the rain …'

'Stop shouting.' White lipped, she shrinks further into the corner and draws deeply on a fresh cigarette.

'Oh for god's sake, I'm not shouting. There's no one else here anyway.'

'Those two could repeat every word we've said – and tell you what we had for breakfast.'

'Who, the old dolls at the counter? They're not even looking this way.'

'They're hanging on to every word. That one in the hairnet was. Watching the kids like a hawk. Daring them to make a noise, knock something over.'

'You're imagining things …'

'Oh you – the farm this, the farm that. You never notice what's going on around you!' She grinds the half-finished cigarette into the ashtray.

Rob shakes his head, 'so what if they are listening? We don't know them. We're never likely to see them again …'

'I just hate busybodies! I'm fed up with all this, this … what are we doing? Camping grounds, public toilets, public bars, Paragon Cafes – Susan telling everyone we eat Weetbix for tea and live in a caravan …'

'Oh love,' Rob laughs, but his voice is concerned, 'come on.'

'We're living like gypsies!'

'Look, I thought we agreed it was no use stopping till we find the right spot – till we know we can make a go of it. Crikey, it should be a holiday. We should be having the time of our lives. You'll probably look back on this in ten years' time and wish you could do it all again.' Margaret greets this with a withering look. He shrugs, 'the kids are having a whale of a time. And who cares what other people think, love? It doesn't matter!'

'I care,' she says quietly. 'It does matter. I'm sick of it all. And I'm sick of talking about it.'

Susan and Cathy burst in from the now sunny street. 'The Station Master showed us how the signal box works, and how messages come through.'

'And a lady had lunch with us. She liked my jumper …'

' … And she said my hair's pretty …'

Yes, thinks Margaret, *and her husband put thirty years of their life into a farm that ended up killing him.*

'Good girls. I think we might see about some ice creams, eh? We'll walk up to the lighthouse later, blow the cobwebs away.'

Cathy wriggles onto Rob's knee, 'Are we going to live here, Dad?'

'Lots more adventures to go yet. What say we have a look at the map tonight and you can choose where we stay next …'

From the wind-ravaged headland they see the approaching train. 4.11. Watch it snaking round to the next bay, lead by a plume of smoke; hear the shrill whistle and the hiss of steam as the heavy, iron, south-rolling wheels of the North Coast Mail screech to a halt.

Margaret pictures Mrs. Timmins: settling into her carriage, luggage and overcoat stowed in the netted shelf above, fussing with the rug, lowering the table for her packed refreshments and knitting, sinking gratefully into the high-backed seat. Gazing out the window as the train gathers speed. Going back home.

23

She smoothes her hand over the sixpenny booklet Mrs. Timmins left behind. It's in her shoulder bag, along with her cigarettes and *The Grapes of Wrath*: "Department of Railways/New South Wales. TIMETABLE – COUNTRY SERVICES From 25th November 1951".

McClaren's Ridge, February 1954

CATHY

MUM'S IN THE bedroom feeling pale, saying what else can go wrong in this godforsaken place. We've got a new baby coming and Mr. Robinson's at the back door telling Dad there might be another cyclone on the way and Dad's saying swear words because we're still waiting on that iron sheeting and Susan wants to know if we can go and stay with Robinsons again.

This place is McClaren's Ridge. There are lots of things that grow here with funny names, and lots of things that stick to you and that you shouldn't eat. But you can suck honey out of the lantana flowers and eat the wild raspberries. Sometimes we get splinters, but except for school we hardly ever have to wear shoes.

It was a long time in the Chev getting here and we did have some adventures on the way, but a lot of days Dad would have to say stop fidgeting you two and look at the scenery. You could only see it if it was your turn to sit near the window though and mostly it wasn't scenery but only grass and trees.

We are on a farm and now I'm in first class. There aren't many crops yet, but millions of scotch thistles and lantana and stinking roger that you have to get rid of with a brush hook. The tomatoes all just got washed away, but the first thing to worry about was a floor.

Me and Susan had to keep sleeping in the caravan until we got some floor in the old house and no rain coming through the roof where our bedrooms would be. That was all right because we didn't have to pack the beds away every morning, just make them, and when Mum and Dad's bedroom in the house was ready we had a bunk each, instead of me sleeping at the other end of the same one and Susan pretending she was asleep but putting her feet in my face all the time. Which it was like all the way up from Melbourne.

We've got beds in the house now, but sometimes when I wake up my head is down the bottom of the bed with my feet out on the pillow, just like in the caravan.

It's still a bit dangerous to stand on the verandah but you can see right out to the ocean from our hill.

If you look across the flats before the sun comes up, sometimes we have mist and it all looks like a huge dish of white fairy floss with just the tops of the big trees poking out and then Lovett's hill and the sea out at the edge. The grass is a bit cold and silvery, but I pretend that I'm washing my feet in the dew the way fairies do. Even the stinking roger and the cobbler's pegs look pretty with diamond drops all along the cobwebs and on the tops of the paspalum that sparkle when the sun comes out. And then you see the underneath world when the clouds lift up and the cows are all standing round eating and looking as if to say ha-ha, we were here all the time.

Mostly when we need groceries and things we might go with the Robinsons when Harry goes into Kalinga in the Dodge. That was a godforsaken time for Mum last year because it was so hot in November Ernie Lovett said you could fry an egg in the road, and Mum had to climb in the back with morning sickness and a good dress and everything. All the front seat in Robinson's truck was full because Beth Robinson is an air-hostess now and doesn't like getting her hair messed up, and when they got to town Harry forgot Mum was back there, so right in the middle of Oxley Street she had to yell out for him to let her out and then try to get down with all the people in the street looking.

But I hope we don't get a new cyclone, because that was the most godforsaken thing by far. When we had it the baby wasn't ready to come for a month, but god forbid it might come at any time and the hospital is way down in Booralla and we already had floods.

Before Dad found this farm we went swimming all the time but now we're in the country and the Ute's on its last legs and it keeps raining. But you don't moan and groan about the rain because now the new tanks are full. That was something else that had to be worried about when we got here, because they didn't work. Mum looked in one, all rusty with holes, and said oh my god and Dad said it's nothing, but Susan says she bets it was a snake. They like places like that to sleep through the winter she said. So Dad has fixed the tanks and the floor and just as well, but the roof is still something to worry about.

At first all the rain was good, but then things started getting washed away, cows and banana stools and everything. They are called stools instead of trees. Dad said we'd be apples being up high but Mum said she was going back to Grandma's place in Sydney. The roads got flooded and boats got smashed and waves came right over the street in Kalinga. There wasn't a dry piece of washing in the house and red mud all over the good floor.

We stayed home from school for a whole week. On Friday they said the rain was going out to sea, but the next day the radio station stopped working and Harry Robinson came to tell us it was a Cyclone. It was coming back again that night to hit Kalinga he said. Dad said damn and blast, we're not ready for this I don't think the roof will hold. Ernie Lovett said it looked like being the biggest one he'd ever seen and he'd seen a few.

It got really windy again and the roof was already banging on one corner, so Dad went up to try and nail it down, but that made Mum worry more because he would blow off. It started raining hard again anyway and the lamps kept going out and you couldn't keep the side verandah dry because except for Susan's part it hasn't got proper walls yet. So we shut the doors and tried to go to bed.

We might have been asleep for a while, but then the wind woke us up and it was even louder and scarier than the storm at Shell Bay. Jacaranda branches were flying round the yard and rain blew in through the gaps in the back door. Mum and Dad were trying to get us all to a part of the house that might be safe. Then another big booming noise started, even louder than the wind. It was just like the drums at the Anzac Day parade. Dad said we had to get out of there before the roof went and we were going up to Robinsons who have a sturdy house and a proper roof. Maybe some already blew away, but then there was this huge crunch and even louder banging and no time to stand around.

Mum thought it would be worse outside. She said it's three o'clock in the morning, we can't just all roll up at this hour and Dad said for heaven's sake they'd be furious if we didn't, you don't think they'll be sleeping through this do you and Susan said you'd have to be dead to be sleeping through this. We had to go down the front verandah steps, which were still dangerous, and help Mum but not fall through, because if we went out the back door one of the mango trees might hit us.

We had blankets and raincoats wrapped around us but they all blew up anyway and we just got drenched. It didn't even look like night-time. There was so much wind and so much lightning, one minute the sky was black and then all glary. Wet leaves were stuck all over us and the rain was so sharp it made your face hurt. It was very hard to even stand up straight and keep walking but we had to try not to slip over and we had to hurry in case Mum had the new baby right there in the road. It felt as if we were trying to get to Robinsons for two days, but Mr. and Mrs. Robinson and Harry and

April were still up when we got there and happy to see us in one piece.

Here we are Dad said, all the drowned rats. Mrs Robinson said Oh Margaret love you're soaked to the bone. Mum looked funny with gumboots full of water and clothes all stuck to her and that big round tummy all wet. Come and get yourself dried off love, she said the last thing we need is for you to be catching a chill so close to time. We all got dried off and April Robinson made cups of cocoa. We'd never been up so late but no one was sleepy.

Mr. Robinson and Harry and Dad were all talking about the damage. It's a beauty all right Mr. Robinson said, worst I've seen, be lucky if that place of yours is still there tomorrow Rob and Mrs. Robinson said Wal, for heavens sake, it's bad enough for poor Margaret already. After we had got warmed up April took us into her room and Susan and I both got into Beth's bed, but the same way up. We didn't sleep a wink before it was time to get up again.

All the flat was under water when we walked out to see from the top of the ridge and our house looked crooked over on the next hill. Still standing Dad said. Mum said she was sorry it didn't blow away. You could see through all the trees but the sun was out again and everything looked washed and clean and Mum didn't have the baby too soon. The trees are hanging out to dry I said and Mrs. Robinson said that's right Little Dot so I poked my tongue out at Susan and April because they thought that was funny.

There is still biggest ever flooding and we can stay home from school for a while and it's all hands on deck with cleaning up the mess and getting a decent roof over our heads. Mum didn't go to Sydney, and it's too late now because of the baby still coming and Susan says this is a sub tropical climate so there will be lots of storms.

The Queen came before the cyclone.

I wanted to see her but she didn't come to McClaren's Ridge or even Kalinga. The kindergarten kids were too small to go, but Susan saw her over in Hartley and it was so wet that when she got home all her skin was blue from her tunic. Mum said Jesus wept what were they thinking about, you'll all catch your deaths.

Well Susan didn't catch her death but she did see the Queen, which I didn't. And I don't think I'll ever find my other gumboot.

In the cyclone I had to stop and try to empty the water out and Dad said what on earth are you doing leave it or we'll all drown. Susan said he didn't mean leave it there, but I did and it must have blown away to Booralla or somewhere. I put the one that didn't blow away in the back verandah cupboard. I think probably they were a bit too small for me, so I might need a new pair anyway. Before the next cyclone comes.

SUSAN

WELL, SHE'D BEEN to see the Queen. Except that she didn't go down with Alice and it wasn't Buckingham Palace. Millions of school kids all went down on the bus and it was in Hartley and it rained. Everyone said she was one of the world's most beautiful women; that her skin was just so white it looked like a painting, and Prince Phillip was very handsome. But you had to stand on tiptoe to look, and even then it was hard because of all the umbrellas. The Royal Car was very black and shiny.

"The most memorable event in North Coast history" it said the next day in the paper, but nobody mentioned that they might all end up with pneumonia. Or that their underwear would never be white again because everything was stained from their tunics. She had a whole navy belt tattooed around her waist when she got undressed. And hands blue with cold, all day, right from the time she got off the bus in Hartley. 'Which wasn't supposed to happen up here, Dad,' she said.

When he decided they were leaving the city he said the north coast would be better because in Melbourne it was always cold and raining. Well, that was a laugh. Just after the first Christmas, when Dad picked McClaren's Ridge as the right spot, thunder and storms every afternoon just about. Then the same all through last summer. And now this year, a real cyclone. "Black February" the papers said. And they were calling the area "Cyclone Alley", because cyclones had been coming through all along the coast right down from Bundaberg. And now there was probably another one coming. It was Shell Bay all over again. Only worse. It wasn't as if they could pack up and leave now.

And even though they were finally on a farm, she'd just about given up the ghost on any Friend Flicka. An actual horse to ride was something that might happen when their ship came in. The Ship being what Dad said about everything they needed. But she was pretty sure that if it did come, the ship would be bringing a tractor for all of them (ha- ha), before a horse for her. They could ride Bessie, the Lovett's draught horse. She had that lovely warm fur and straw smell, but all she ever did was plod around. And she'd looked about ready to give up the ghost after Dad borrowed her to plough up the front paddock.

That was for the first crop. They'd been looking forward to passionfruit pies, but a hailstorm flattened all the vines last Christmas. Well, lucky the mulberry tree and the lemons were still there. They were growing wild anyway, left over from whoever had the farm before Mum and Dad. It used to be a dairy farm, but Dad was supposed to be growing small crops. It had been tomatoes this year, but they'd gone west too, washed down the hill in a storm. Cathy said maybe they could try big crops.

He wanted to try beans and bananas next, but there was more ploughing to do. 'Bananas', Mum said, 'I thought you'd decided they were too much. What about your back?'

'We haven't got much choice love', he said. 'We have to put something in that isn't going to get washed away in the first rainstorm. They're the best bet at the market now.'

Mum said she thought the prices were high because all the plantations got ruined in the cyclone. He'd be ploughing round the hill instead of up and down, he said, but now wasn't the time to argue about it.

Dad used to talk about how when they got settled they'd be able to go to the beach all the time, but now the Chev was sold and all they had was this old bomb Ford that was broken down half the time and they could only go on weekends. When there wasn't much work to do. Which actually meant never, because you never saw anything like the mess the farm was when they first got there.

Just as well they'd had the caravan, because you couldn't stay in the old house. Well, it looked like a house from the outside, but there wasn't any glass in the windows and just about no floor. And you didn't know what might be living in the roof because there were holes everywhere. Even now that they'd moved into their bedrooms, sometimes at night it sounded as if there were little bunches of carpenters hammering and sawing up in the ceiling. She said to Dad 'Well, can I have a possum if we can't afford a horse', but he just said 'You'd be sorry'.

So almost the whole of the first year of their new improved life was spent with Dad building a floor so they could start living in the house. And the rest of them chopping wood. Well they still had to do that. You wanted things like a horse and you got a tomahawk with a ribbon round the handle for Christmas. And one Arthur Mee's Encyclopedia. There were ten in the set, but they got one every Christmas, which meant she'd be nearly finished school before there was an index. They needed to get the combustion stove going for hot water, so she took turns with Mum to cut kindling and some of the small logs, and Cathy bundled it up. And whinged. They only had an ice chest now too, instead of a refrigerator, so the iceman had to come with big blocks of ice wrapped in hessian bags, and they got milk straight from the cows next door.

Lovett's farm was still a dairy. She and Cathy walked across in the afternoons after school. They'd watch if the boys were still milking, or sometimes go in and talk to Gran. She'd had her own poddy calf to raise when she was little. 'Me and Iris McClaren,' she said, 'we'd be walking to school and Bluebell would follow us. They let her wait in the yard till the bell went.' Iris McClaren was Mrs. Robinson's name before she got married. They'd been best friends then. 'That's another story, love,' Gran said.

But the cyclone and the Queen were about the most exciting things that had happened since they'd got to McClaren's Ridge. And now they had Tom.

They'd nearly missed the Queen altogether because of the weather, but her visit came in between their cyclone and the ones up north, so even though it almost got cancelled, it wasn't. High school classes from everywhere went to represent the North Coast Area. Of course the Tour was going to Brisbane, but Hartley was a special stop so people in the country could see her. The papers said that before she came out from the Palace, her Majesty had *"particularly asked to have every opportunity to see the country's children"*.

The day of the visit was the tenth of February, and they'd made it a public holiday, so all the shops would be closed. At school in the week before that, Susan's class had a time each day where they read out pieces that they'd brought in from the newspapers. About the Royal Tour.

All the kids were dying to see Hartley, because the Gazette said there were already special displays lit up in the main street shop windows. There was a picture of one that had a huge crown with hanging gardens all around it, with palm trees and flowers. It said some were artificial, but mainly fresh cut ones that they had to change every day! There were going to be five brass bands and two pipe bands that would "take up positions from 8am and play continuously till the Queen's departure". There were to be "2,500 children from 81 schools". They'd all be assembled in Pines Oval, with lanes wide enough for the royal car to drive through, which was scheduled for twenty past ten. Then she would drive back through the town and head for Morrisbrook at ten forty five.

There had been meetings of the Royal Tour Committee ever since the Coronation. Trying to decide things like whether the whole choir would sing *God Save Our Gracious Queen* or just the best singers, and who could recite *I Love a Sunburnt Country*. And where everyone would meet to catch the bus and how many buses to book.

In the end it hadn't mattered, because it rained so much that most of the entertainment had to be cancelled. What mainly happened was that they'd all stood around waiting and getting wet, in straight rows.

All the committees had been pretty desperate by the Monday, two days before Her Majesty was due, because that was when "cyclones were lashing 500 miles of Queensland coast". They had a special train standing by at Newcastle to take the Queen and Duke to Hartley if there was "danger of flooding or conditions got too unfavourable for flying". On Tuesday, there was "torrential rain" in Fishers Wharf where the plane was meant to be landing at 8.15 the next morning, and they were making other plans. But in the end the Royal Party got through all right, and all the school kids went to the Oval and lined up. Leaving room for the Royal Car. The trouble was, the ground was too boggy, so they just had to drive around the outside on the running track, and because of the rain they couldn't use an open-topped car like they'd had in Sydney.

Still, the bus ride home was fun.

Cathy got the sulks. 'Susan keeps talking like newspapers, Mum.'

And when everyone was celebrating the Coronation last year, the Kindergarten kids had this competition. Cathy drew the best crown, and so she was picked to be the pretend Queen Elizabeth. She had to choose a Prince Philip from the boys, and they'd put on dress-up cloaks and acted out the Coronation procession in the playground in front of the whole Infants school. 'So I should be seeing the Queen,' she said. But the infants' classes were too little and there were already so many kids organised to go that no-one knew how they were all going to fit into the Oval.

Afterwards, in the Kalinga Gazette, it said that there were eleven thousand children. The Royal Party even drove twice around the Oval instead of just once, which was expected. And they stayed five minutes longer than they were meant to because there were so many people.

Mrs. Robinson had gone over with the Red Cross ladies. She said it just brought tears to everyone's eyes at the Base Hospital, because they'd wheeled the bed-ridden patients out onto the footpath so they could see the Queen too, and the Royal Car even stopped on the wrong side of the road and everything, just so she could put her head out the window and chat to them.

'Gee,' Cathy said, 'their beds would be all wet.' Susan had been thinking the same thing, but she didn't say it.

'Oh, no love,' Mrs Robinson said, 'they were in wheelchairs. The nurses were all holding umbrellas. You know, over the chairs. It was lovely.'

Actually, when the Queen was in Sydney it had been very hot and people were passing out all over the place, so she might have been happy that it rained.

And she definitely would have been glad to get out when she did.

There had been temporary relief from flooding for a day or so, but then there were landslides, cattle wandering about, roads cut, and "thousands of acres of farmland and cane fields under water". Then on the thirteenth of February, "monsoon winds strengthened and sent a new cyclone threat sweeping south."

That just kept up for a week. Dad had been trying to finish fixing up the house, but with all the rain and so much to do it was just hopeless. So they ended up having a cyclone adventure at three o'clock in the morning. It was amazing, except that Mum thought she might have the baby in the middle of it all. And she doesn't even like coming out of the bedroom in a thunderstorm. They'd had to get out of the house in case it just collapsed, and walk all the way to Robinson's in the dark. And a piece of the roof did blow off.

There was so much water. Sudden little rivers out of nowhere tearing down the gravel road and swirling round in the mud gully. Susan could almost imagine they were the only people in the world, or they were on another planet with this weird coloured weather. The wind sounded like a million trucks. 'Hold my hand,' Dad had said. He'd started off with her on one side, Mum on the other and Cathy on his shoulders, but that was impossible. It was just too hard to stay together. Then there'd been this enormous flare of lightning, and everything looked so bright she'd felt like someone was taking a giant flash bulb family photo. But you could see Mum's face in that light. She'd gone white as a sheet. She screamed, and grabbed her stomach and sort of crumpled down in the road.

They all stopped, but Dad yelled, 'Go on! Go on with Cathy. Hold the blanket!' he said, 'hold the blanket and hold Cathy's hand. Don't let go of each other.' Then he nearly went crazy because Cathy was trying to tip water out of one of her gumboots. 'Don't worry about that!' He was shouting, but the wind almost blew the words away, 'Just keep going! And hold on to Susan!' It was easier to go in bare feet because they knew where the smooth parts of the road were, but trying to hold onto the blanket was like being in a tug of war with the other team invisible. Just not flying away was hard.

It was the worst in the area's history. (Northern New South Wales. Just. They were always having to tell relations from the city that they didn't live in Queensland, but right on the border. There wasn't a street name or a number, just a road in McClaren's Ridge, via Kalinga, the Far North Coast, New South Wales, Australia, the World, the Universe. There was even a border fence with gates going through to the next state). Twenty houses had been destroyed, people were caught in trees, boats and cars were washed out to sea, and people had found snakes in their cupboards.

If they'd stayed in the house and those mangoes and jacarandas had come down, they'd all be dead, but except for a compost heap of branches and leaves where the yard used to be, the trees were still standing. The house was too, except for the roof. But Susan knew she was especially lucky. After they'd got to Robinson's and Mrs. Robinson had got Mum comfortable and all the youngsters were tucked up, there had been a bit of a lull in the wind and she heard Dad talk to Mr. Robinson about going back down to the old house. He didn't want Mum to know he was going, but he'd remembered some other stuff that needed tying down. Then, she had no idea how much later it was, but the wind and rain had woken her and she could hear Dad's voice again, 'Thank God we left when we did,' he was saying, 'south side's a mess. The side verandah windows've blown in. Great sheets of broken glass everywhere.'

Her bed had been right under those windows. A couple of days later, she actually heard Ernie Lovett say, 'By jingoes Rob, that was the eye of the storm you were out in,' so she guessed that meant someone had been watching out for Dad too. And touch wood, there hadn't been any more cyclones. Black February was over. It looked as if they would have to think up another colour for March.

And now there were five Williamses. According to Dad, it didn't only rain cats and dogs; it had rained a baby brother. The house seemed to be full of wet nappies but he was beautiful and everyone was happy. Tiny little toes and fingers he had, and soft hair that stood up all over his head like a dandelion puff, although Mum said that would probably fall out. Thomas David Williams, but he would be Tom.

Just before he'd been born, all the shops in Booralla and Hartley had big flood sales. "Right Royal Values" for stock that had only been slightly damaged, and a lot of it was all right. Dad got the old jalopy going and they all got dressed up to go over to Hartley on a shopping trip, so Cathy didn't miss out altogether. They got some nice extra blankets and pillowcases and a good little bassinet so Mum could take Tom up to the shed or out in the car. Next time it decided to start, that is. They'd already had the bunny rug, but now Tom also had his own small blanket.

The Manchester and Bedding sales seemed to be the main thing. Maybe because other things could be dried out and you couldn't tell if they'd been in the flood or not.

Dad said 'They'll be able to fix up all those wet hospital beds now.' Just another one of his corny jokes.

Part Two

Just like
a real home

"The best
Thing we can do is to make wherever we're lost in
Look as much like home as we can."
Christopher Fry, 'The Lady's Not for Burning'

McClaren's Ridge, May 1954

MARGARET

THE WOOD IS resisting the axe. The clothes came out of the copper earlier today still stained with red mud, which she now knows will never come out. It's getting cooler and the dark will come suddenly and still there is no fire lit for hot water, and she doesn't feel like cooking a meal for anyone, or eating it. Her breasts are sore and swollen, her nose is running, she has no handkerchief in the pocket of her skirt and the backs of her hands would leave her face streaked with sawdust and soot.

She had thought things couldn't get worse. "As god is my witness" - it is no longer amusing to imagine herself as Scarlett, faced with the challenge of a pillaged Tara – "as god is my witness, I'll never" – never what? Spend another day in a house that might blow away with the next strong breeze? Spend weeks planting a crop, their first, to see all those eager rows of fresh green tomato shoots washed down the hill? Get pregnant so she can lie in the road in the eye of a storm to be lashed by cyclonic wind and rain and possibly sliced through by a flying piece of their own roof just weeks before the baby is due?

She'll go back to Sydney. A sleeping berth when Tom is a few months older maybe, onto solids. Take Cathy and Susan, and the baby; leave Rob to get his damn farm going. If there is ever going to be a way to do that – she's seen no evidence. Their life seems to be governed by bad news followed by worse news. Bad weather followed by forecasts of worse weather. Bad market prices followed by falling market prices. No time to do anything about the house, followed by no money to do anything.

She had a letter from Sydney yesterday. She knows that's what's brought the black mood on, but too bad. She's torn between looking forward to hearing from the family and the fact that it just makes everything worse. She never seems to have the time to write to anyone, and when she does, it's an exercise in making something appalling sound like a good choice: the far north coast – sunshine, life on the farm – great place to bring up the kids.

She'll never forget the first time Rob brought them out to see McClaren's Ridge – *I've found the spot, love* … About a month after they'd arrived at Kalinga – idyllic times then for her and the girls – the clear days and cool nights of September and October, as close to spring as you came up here. They were still camping at the beach – one long holiday – but he'd found work, had to, almost immediately, cutting and packing bananas. Home just before dark, filthy, covered in black sap and dog tired, back stiffer every morning – all the pain of an injury sustained in a wartime forced crash landing reawakened – at the same time keeping an ear to the ground for a likely farm to buy … *fifty odd acres on a hilltop about five miles west of Kalinga, perfect north-easterly aspect.*

The drive out there was pleasant. Houses becoming sparser past the outskirts of the town, then the rather alarming crossing of a rickety jumble of boards that announced itself as Whipbird Creek Bridge: passage for no more than one vehicle at a time, with a distinct dip in the middle. When they finally reached the far side of the river, the unsealed road wound a further mile or two up the hill, shaded by pockets of rainforest, no signs of habitation till they reached the corrugated iron mailbox that marked the turn off to McClaren's Ridge. And then only the three houses: on the first rise, a comfortable looking, freshly painted timber farmhouse surrounded by huge old Moreton Bay Figs, Hoop Pines, Camphor Laurels and green paddocks; another, in the distance, similarly neat and well cared for, visible when you crested the hill. And between the two, an abandoned dairy farm. Their prospective home.

'Land's perfect – fantastic views' ... well, she didn't know the first thing about farming, but yes, the view took your breath away. 'There's even a house on it – needs a bit of work'... she'd draw a veil over that one. The jacarandas, three huge trees that must have been older than the house, were in full bloom, glowing canopies of lavender blossom, seemingly growing out of a purple carpet – it looked like something out of a Victorian collection of illustrated fairy stories – and a row of enormous, gnarled mango trees further up the hill, behind the house.

'We'll put the new house up there, above the mangoes. Fruit laid on,' he said. 'It's a little Garden of Eden – mangoes, mulberries, there's even a custard apple tree and a persimmon, a dam the kids can use as a swimming hole. We'll get the farm up and running first,' he said, 'this old joint will be fine till we get established. Just need a few new sheets of roofing iron. Arthur says we can get second-hand timber from the mill to fix the floor. And the CSR's selling off some old Yank Army surplus stuff – Ford Utes going for a song. I'll sell the Chev and we'll have extra cash for timber and farm supplies to get started ...'

She'd tried to fight off a blanket of fatigue, disappointment and anxiety. This was obviously home already as far as Rob was concerned. She'd turned to the view, held on to the words 'new house', but all she could think was, how could she ever unpack all their china, books, vases, pictures – things wrapped so carefully at the other end with a new home in mind, into this hollow shell of raw boards, rusted iron and empty doorframes ... 'neighbours on either side ...'

Ah – the neighbours. Ernie Lovett is terrific; generous, funny, the kids love him, and Mrs. Robinson, Harry, April, she doesn't know how she'd have survived this far without the Robinsons.

But the rest of them – and the fact that there is still some age old feud still festering between the Lovetts and the Robinsons, with the Williams family located, at least geographically, right in the middle, makes for problems unlooked for in light of the day to day struggle that is already life in McClaren's Ridge. She feels as though she's not being allowed to join a club she doesn't want to belong to anyway.

You do things the way they always did. Good enough for your father and his father before him and how long have they been farming this district. You know what to do because the family was brought up to it - oh, she knows what they're saying – *One cocky bloke from down south, with a couple of rich friends in Booralla, thinks he knows it all, big plans, riding for a fall that Rob Williams. And her, she might have read a lot and have lots of smart city clothes, but she's got another think coming out here.*

Well, they're probably right. Or they've won. She doesn't care. Well, she does care. Rob doesn't. And that's the difference. They've been here two years now, and she still feels like a stranger.

They'd been thrilled to get the invitation to Allan Robinson's wedding. Margaret said they'd love to go, but while Susan was quite capable of looking after Cathy, Tom was too young to be left, still needing four hourly feeds. 'Bring him along, love,' said Mrs. Robinson, 'you must come – chance to get out, kick up your heels with the young ones. There'll be plenty of girls on hand to look after him.'

Allan was their oldest son, marrying Helen, a plump, pretty girl who had grown up on a dairy farm, had no desire to be anything other than a dairy farmer's wife, and whose wedding day would be the most glorious and terrifying day of her life. She'd been Allan's girlfriend since about sixth class. They'd got engaged just after her debut, and what with the glory box, the engagement party, and the rounds of shower teas and hen's nights, Helen had amassed about enough bed linen, napery, crockery, cutlery and cookware to furnish three farmhouses.

A country wedding, they'd looked forward to it – Margaret for the chance to dress up in something other than shorts and shed clothes, both of them because it seemed a sort of unofficial acceptance of them as part of the community.

Tiny wooden church, fresh painted cream and white, reception at Acacia Flats Hall, streamers, flowers, catering by the Presbyterian Ladies' Auxiliary – yards of plywood trestle tables, starched white cloths and cross-stitched, cut-work doilies almost hidden beneath mountains of cream cakes, iced sponges, fruit salad, huge, perspiring cut-glass punch bowls filled with shimmering liquid, quivering trifles, carefully arranged vol-au-vents, pies, pasties, cold chicken, coleslaw.

All the young farmers, shy boys with sunburnt faces and white foreheads under slicked back hair, shoes polished and creaking, dancing the Barn Dance, the Pride of Erin, the Gypsy Tap, some awkwardly, others surprisingly graceful and light on their feet. Lighter on their feet as the night wore on, more raucous and braver, no more wallflowers left and if they weren't dancing as couples they just formed a big boisterous circle and thundered up and down the hall.

Rob had been in his element, dancing with each of the ladies who had taken it upon themselves to rock Tom's bassinet, talking crop salvage and caterpillar plagues. And Margaret loved dancing; had soon relaxed enough to stop feeling overdressed in her Mark Foy's top floor dress, and not feel embarrassed that she'd been a nuisance having to bring Tom.

But she remembered the speeches – Helen's father, beaming and red-faced – 'Unaccustomed as I am', countless giggling sisters and cousins snorting and rolling their eyes every time he'd hinted at anything to do with married bliss and the possibility of family additions – 'very proud to be able to call Allan our son-in-law', he said, 'but very sorry that Helen's marrying out of the district …'

My god, she'd thought, Helen and Allan were both born in Booralla Hospital. Acacia Flat was the next valley north from McClaren's Ridge. They would be settling on Alan's allotted parcel of the Robinson farm, fifteen acres on the northwest corner butting onto the next 'district'.

And Rob thinks we're locals.

McClaren's Ridge, 1955

CATHY

IT'S GOOD WHEN I can go with Dad to the saw mill on Saturdays. Especially when Susan has got friends out to visit. She lets me do things with them but they don't really want me to and all they ever talk about is horses anyway.

Dad doesn't need wood for fixing up the house anymore but we still go to the mill for the packing cases. It's way up at Cutter's Glen and Dad had to ask Harry if we could borrow the Dodge. I like the smell of the wood and running your feet through the little hills of sawdust, all tiny curls like powder on the top but further in damp and smelling like our camphor chest that came up from Melbourne and sticking to your toes. And when they cut the ends off the planks and logs you get a pile of little neat blocks with all different patterns on the sides. Cutter, well his name is really Mr. Cooper but everyone calls him Cutter, said to Dad, your little girl's got a good tan there. Well ha-ha.

I've really got this white skin and freckles, but Mum rubbed on some special tan stuff to dye my skin for last night which is still on because I didn't have time to scrub my arms and legs and everything and there was no time to put my hair in plaits, which was good because I hate having the knots brushed out. We had to leave early so Robinsons can have their car back to go to town for the groceries.

It was the Fancy Dress Ball. I went as a Hawaiian Girl with proper frangipanis in my hair and around my neck that Mum and I

48

threaded together and a bowl with a pineapple and proper bananas in it and a piece of flowery material wrapped around me that I was a bit worried would fall down. It didn't but I didn't win either, and Cheryl Pryce got a prize for a Hula Girl and she just had on a fake grass skirt and plastic flowers. Dad said my outfit was more Orthentic but they wouldn't know. He's been to Fiji.

Mum fixed up a lovely taffeta dress that she used to wear for parties in Melbourne for Susan as Belle of the Ball with a velvet sash and gloves and everything. She didn't win either but I thought she looked really orthentic too.

Mum's dress was one of the things we unpacked when our ship came in. Well it wasn't really our ship but I thought it might be. I was running down to the mailbox one day when Susan stayed to talk to Gran Lovett because our Grandma's Christmas parcel would be coming from Sydney soon, and I heard this really loud engine noise coming up the quarry road. I knew it wasn't the carrier because it was the wrong day and we didn't have any tomatoes ready to go and then I saw this enormous brown truck coming up around the hill. It turned out it wasn't really brown, it was just dirty and when it got closer I could see writing in the white rivery lines running through the red mud pattern on the sides and letters that said R_CE __ROS EMOV _ LS. I didn't think I could remember many things about Melbourne, but the truck made me think about all the big tea chests and the fluffy piles of paper strips that got packed in to make sure things didn't break and then the men rolling everything into the back of it with little sort of wheelbarrow things. So I ran all the way home and said our ship's coming and everyone laughed.

Christmas is always a bit like the ship. Susan and me might be getting bikes this year because of the pineapples, so then we won't have to walk all the way down to Whipbird Creek to catch the bus. Dad got a new tractor too so he got the bulldozers to make another paddock over on the back hill which is where he put the pineapples. They grew properly so things are looking up around here Dad said.

Cutter's Sawmill is where we got all the wood for the kitchen bench too that Dad made with shelves at the end for all the special big dishes and pans and speckled green laminex on top. There was some of that left over so one wall in the bathroom is finished too.

Some parts of the house are lovely now and after the floods we all got new mosquito nets for our beds. Just as well Tom got a new blanket too because now that he can walk he takes the old one with him everywhere and he likes to go exploring. As if it didn't get grimy enough on the floor he took it to the bean patch one day and Mum said well that's it. She has to keep washing it but it's a walking blanket now.

I wanted to sleep in my bedroom while it was being painted so I could watch how different it looked each day, but Dad said the fumes would be too strong. I think that's the best part. All the new building smells. And the putty was lovely to press into shapes, like plasticine, but you can't even see it now. It smelt even better than the paint and I wasn't allowed to do much painting, but Dad let me open the new little putty buckets and make the balls and smooth them into the nail holes and stir the paint all lovely at first like cream with stripes through it. Especially the watermelon. And teal.

I didn't know what teal was before, but Susan has that and it's pretty with white on the ceiling. She said there are ducks called teals because of their bluey green feathers. She is on the part of the side verandah that is fixed up but in my bedroom the walls are taller and have a row of wood right round which is for hanging pictures and a lovely scrolly carving of cut out leaves and flowers over the doorway. Dad says all these old houses have those. When I'm in bed I can still see the pattern from the light of the lamp in the lounge room and I try to count how many cut out bits there are but I never get it because you can't remember where you started. We helped pick our own colours off the cards with all the squares of paint in rows so my bedroom has grey but on the top and over the picture rail I got watermelon pink. Which is like a Galah's colours, so we both have sort of bird rooms.

Mum's kitchen is lovely and sunny and all yellow with the polished floor and the lemon tree outside the window. We've even got all things in the cupboards and pictures on the wall and a long bookcase that Dad made in the lounge room and nice new armchairs that were Mum and Dad's present last Christmas. It's just like a real house.

Dad says the bits that aren't finished will be done all in good time. You can still only sit on safe parts of the verandah. When it is fixed up we can put the old car seat out there Dad said. Mum said over my dead body when he said it could be a couch in the lounge room.

SUSAN

'I WON'T ARGUE,' Mum said, what do I know about crank shafts and differentials.' *Though god knows we hear enough about them,* she'd said to her and Cathy and the washing up when Dad went outside. And not arguing about it meant not talking about *anything* for a few days – especially when she saw The Great Bargain, which looked like an old dog from the pets' home that nobody else wanted.

'It only needs to get from A to B' he'd said.

'Will it even do that?' Mum said.

'Of course,' he said, 'these old Army jobs – tough as nails.'

But every time they needed to go somewhere, forty good heaves with the crank wouldn't even get it started and someone would end up all dirty. Dodgy brakes too, so you always had to remember to put chocks under it when it was parked.

That was what happened. No one remembers whose turn it was last time they got out of the car or who was in the car last or who didn't chock up the front wheels properly and no one knows how they could have slipped either, but Susan was on the safe end of the front verandah trying to learn *Daffodils,* when she heard a sort of clunk and saw the car move. At first she wondered who was going out, but there was no engine noise and when the time came for it to turn down the driveway it just kept going straight. The front paddock with the gully at the bottom was dead ahead.

You could almost feel the man with his arm up and the gun standing there, saying *On your marks, get set* … and then it started rolling. Slowly at first – she called out to Mum - Cathy might've been there by then too, she couldn't remember – but it bumped over the ruts at the edge of the driveway, bore down to the end of the yard, just missed the persimmon tree, skimmed over the pickers'

52

path at the top of the paddock, then it was off like a rocket, heading for the bottom and out of sight.

Well you wouldn't have believed if you didn't see it. When it disappeared Cathy kept saying oo-ah, and the two of them were sort of laughing and screaming all at once, but by the time Mum got out from the back verandah she was mainly screaming, 'Where's Rob? Where's your father! Who was in it?' Then as soon as she realised it had just taken off by itself, she said 'You mean to say – you mean to say you just watched the whole thing and didn't do anything?' Well gee, thought Susan, apart from putting on my Superman suit and flying down to pick the car up half way down, I don't know what I was supposed to *do*. But it's too late now, and the worst thing is no car at *all* for who knows how long. And probably weeks more of not arguing about it.

She and Cathy went down to the gully with Dad to have a look. Just at the edge of the scrub before the creek, there was an old rock road that Dad says the Kanakas built when they grew cane on the farm before it was a dairy. Well the Ute had flipped right over that by the looks, and landed flat on its back in the creek. Smashed.

'No fixing that,' Dad said. 'Damn.'

Tom was riding on his shoulders. 'Damn,' he said. 'Damn car, Dad.'

He already knew car and Dad, but damn was a new one. He tried it out all the way back up the hill and Mum didn't even tell him it was a naughty word. She agreed with him.

They did get a new couch out of it. The Lovett boys had all come charging down to the gully because they saw it going and thought Dad was in it.

'Good seat there,' Ernie said, 'Plenty of life left in that seat.'

So later on they helped Dad pull the seat out. It looked all right now that it was polished up, but the sooner it moved out of the lounge room the better, according to Mum.

Lovetts' lounge and the armchairs were all a set. They were velvet and so were the curtains on the doors that led out to the verandah. Their house wasn't like *Malua*, up on stilts, so all their hedges and garden trees made the lounge room a bit dark. But it was cosy. It always smelt of roast dinners and Old Pa's tobacco.

Sometimes, when she was walking across for the milk, she'd pretend that's where she lived and that she was coming home after a long journey, or wandering "lonely as a cloud". Yesterday, when the wind was strong and dandelions were blowing through the air and the clouds looked like streaming horses' tails, she was a mixture of Van Gogh outside in France painting the clouds and the Highwayman riding up to the old inn door; (the Lovett's bails were the stables behind the inn), Sir Francis Drake laid his cloak down for her to step across the sloppy strip of mud and manure that led to the bails. Even in the dry, it was like she supposed quicksand must be, with all those brown milky hoof holes. Dad had got some cows now too, but for beef, not milking. A tractor too, but still no sign of a horse.

Ernie gave her a go at milking a couple of times and she could do it, but her arms got tired pretty quickly. Old Pa's hands were permanently curled up, as if he was milking cows all the time. She loved just being there and watching – the smell of the warm milk and leather reins hanging on the wall nails and the men's boots and sweaty hats and the cows' bellies and the clang of the buckets. Then that furry slap on their rumps before they clattered and slid out of their stalls onto the wet concrete, jumped down into the bog, struggled up to dry grass and back out to the paddock.

Then the boys poured that new frothy milk, almost yellow, into the buckets through a muslin cloth to keep the dirt out. She and

54

Mum always tried to keep the new milk till the next day. By that time you could almost peel off the layer of cream that had come to the top and it was the most delicious thing, whipped up with bananas and passionfruit. Or pineapple.

She'd brought a pineapple to give to Gran. When she went in, Gran was settled with her feet up on a little tapestry footstool that she'd sewed before her eyes went and peeling potatoes in her lap. Listening to the radio serial – 'They'll never get together,' she said, 'it's just not meant to be. Happy ever after's just for the fairytales.' She turned off the radio when the ending music came on.

'I had a sweetheart once,' she was still looking at the potatoes – 'lovely he was, real handsome. Twice as tall as me but that didn't matter.' Just about everyone would be twice as tall as Gran – 'but his family, and our family, the War – well, in the end, nothing you can do. It's sad you know, and all a bit silly, but there you are. It's little things like that . .'

Susan couldn't believe "That" might've been something to do with all the trouble between the Lovetts and the Robinsons, but later, she told Mum what Gran had said, and Mum said 'Well, you'd be amazed how much trouble land and religion can cause.'

Mc Claren's Ridge, October 1956

CATHY

THE ROBINSONS ARE Presbyterian, the Lovetts are Methodist, and we're not really anything.

We write Church of England on things when there's a space to put religion, because that's what Dad's family was even though he never goes to church and that's the scripture class I go to. Mum was a Roman Catholic but she never goes to Mass either. Susan doesn't care about going to Sunday school much, but all the kids in my class go, so when I'm really good at riding my bike I'm going too.

It doesn't look like any of the Methodist people play tennis. Most of the kids in Acacia Flats go to school there, but some of them must be Catholic because they go on our school bus but they go to St Xavier's school, which everyone calls saint saviours. Well the nuns probably don't. Sometimes Mum will go to play tennis with Harry and the grown up Robinsons on a Saturday arvo. Dad is good but he can't come much because of the farm and there's not enough room till we get another car.

June Lawson had to stop playing again because every time she goes out on to the court her Jamie starts crying again. No tears, just yelling and red in the face. We all try to pat him and tell him it's all right, but he keeps pulling himself up on the wire netting and screams till she comes off. They can't play when he's on there any-way because they might hit him with a tennis ball.

Sometimes Susan and April Robinson have a game, and the rest of us can muck around when they have afternoon tea but we have to borrow our Mum's racquets. I look after Tom but he never cries and he's littler than Jamie Lawson. He just takes his blanket and looks at ants or shows people the flowers and squashed figs he found. He's probably eaten millions so they can't be poisonous. Susan didn't come today because she's at home trying to learn her thank you to the conductor speech for the music concert in Booralla. She always gets picked for things like that because she stands up straight and is beautiful and nearly always comes top of the class or second. She reckons she's nervous but I wouldn't even get picked to start with because I'd just die.

When we were in first class everyone said wait till you get Mrs. Murray. No one likes her, except some of the boys that are her pets. She's got a cranky face and she doesn't believe things. We're starting to learn running writing and I can't do anything properly with my right hand but she says I have to try and we get hit with the ruler all the time, or chalk. I drew a picture of a cat getting married, standing up and wearing a veil and everything like the ones in *Cole's Funny Picture Book* and I didn't get Susan or Dad to help, but she said I must have. And when I told the story about our car running down the hill she said not to make things up.

At least the Acacia Flats kids don't have to have Mrs. Murray.

Why don't youse go to our school, Johnny Lawson said and I didn't know because we are closer to Acacia Flats than to Kalinga. But Mum says it's because of the distrix.

Anyway, I said to him we have a different teacher every year. They only have one teacher for all the kids at their whole school and they have to go to Kalinga anyway when they get to High School. Acacia Flats is like taking the Low Road in the song. After Whipbird Creek you go off round to the flats instead of going up the hill to our place. And the tennis courts are behind Lawson's Store and Acacia Flats Hall. When we first got there every one had to take turns sweeping before they put the net up because the jacaranda flowers had fallen all over the court and it was all slippery and mucky.

There are some picnic tables on one side and a little shed where we have our sandwiches and tea out of thermoses and the ladies take turns to bring slices or a cake. There are stacks of places to play out the back too and trees to climb because there are all the camphor laurels as well as the jacarandas and lots of tunnels where the duranta hedges have grown tall as me nearly. With thorns though, so you have to be careful.

Mum's a good player. She has nice brown legs in her tennis skirt too. Most of the Robinsons are good at tennis. They played ever since they were little. Everyone says Allan and Harry could give Lew Hoad and Frank Sedgeman a run for their money on a good day.

Denny Lovett reckons his Gran was the best tennis player when she was young, but I bet that's a fib. None of the Lovetts play and Gran can't even walk fast with her veins and bunions and everything. But all the Robinson boys and all the Lawsons and Wallaces play so that means there are always heaps of kids to play rounders or marbles or just hideys. We don't know them much but they still let us play.

By the time they start coming to our school there might be a bus right out to McClaren's Ridge or Acacia Flats, but so far there's only one from the other side of Whipbird Bridge. It's a pretty long way to walk but Susan and me can ride our bikes that far and we can leave them at Rogers' Store through the day. And at least you shouldn't get bitten by joe blakes at our school.

Trevor Wallace went swimming in Two Mile Creek for their school sports day and he trod on a black snake. The teacher had to cut his leg to let the blood out and then ride with him all the way to the Ambulance Station in Kalinga in case it got poisonous. I guess all the other kids just had to wait until someone's mother came to look after them and go through their Readers or something.

You hear all sorts of stories at the Sports Club mum says. Susan reckons it could be right about Gran. She said the tennis courts and the distrix and a tragic love story have got something to do with why the Lovetts don't play tennis.

I told all the kids *The Robe* story. It was the first time I was ever allowed to go to the pictures at night and I didn't even get tired. Susan's in love with Victor Mature. I think he looks like he might murder someone with those eyelids, but he was good in the story and she's beautiful. Jean Simmons. They had a special show at the Palace Picture Theatre for *The Robe* being the first Sinimascope picture ever. It was closed for ages to be fixed up and now they have new lights and music and foam rubber seats and this huge new screen that can show Vistavision properly and there's only canvas seats right down the front now.

So it was a big outing for us and lucky because it was just before we lost the old bomb all together.

SUSAN

CATHY SAID, 'WHAT'S a torn akay?'

Susan was in the middle of a good book. The last thing she wanted to do was be a talking dictionary. She turned *Les Miserables* face down in her lap. 'A what?'

'Well, it must be something that you get near the river,' Cathy said, and she told her about Trevor Wallace getting bitten by the snake at Acacia Gully – 'or else it was just really lucky that there was one right there on the bank when they really needed it to save his life.' So she explained about what a tourniquet was and how to spell it.

What next, she thought. But then, just another day in McClaren's Ridge, really.

She was doing French at school now. Last time she'd gone into the School of Arts Library in Booralla with Mum and Cathy, she'd told Miss Elliott about studying French; how much she liked it and how interesting the French Revolution and everything was. She'd asked if there were any books in the library about Napoleon that she might be able to read. Miss Elliott had said, 'I don't know if Napoleon is in this one, but it's a very famous French story about the poor and downtrodden. It is in English though,' she'd said, 'a translation.'

And what a gorgeous little book it was, with an old red leather cover and gold lettering. It actually didn't look that thick, but when she opened it, the pages were like tissue paper and the words so tiny. She was pretty sure she'd never be able to read it without glasses if she was middle-aged or something. "The Miserables" Miss Elliott called it. Mum said she'd need to persevere, but that it was a very good story. So far she was enjoying it, but some days she felt as though it was going to take forever.

And boy, did those people have hard lives; well, the poor ones anyway. But then, when you thought of cyclones wiping out banana plantations one year and an early cold snap making most of them lose their leaves the next, a bridge that sagged in the middle and was just about the only way to get to town, dairy pastures being eaten by caterpillar plagues, kids getting bitten by snakes at swimming lessons, people losing babies before they were even born, because they were trying to lift heavy packing cases, houses that looked like never getting finished because there was just never any money – the thing was, how much worse off were the French?

Maybe Mum was right. Maybe Sydney would be better.

Even the Sydney Symphony Orchestra coming up to the country to play for them was a flop. Well, they came to play for the schools, not just the Williamses. To show how all the instruments worked together; and to help children who wouldn't see symphony orchestras much, appreciate classical music and everything.

The concert wasn't a flop of course, it was beautiful. It was just that she'd been picked to give the thank you speech. It didn't even have to be very long or anything, but even though she'd spent the whole week learning it off by heart, or trying to, she'd been dead scared she'd forget what she'd decided to say. Which was about what happened.

It was down at Booralla, so they'd all gone down in the bus. From the time they left Kalinga, she was trying to remember what she'd practised in front of Mum and Dad and the mirror, and what the conductor's name was, but the more she tried to remember the more her mind went a complete blank.

At the concert, she'd been sitting in the front row to be ready, but for the life of her she couldn't think what pieces had been played as soon as they finished. Which was too bad, because part of the speech had been about how wonderful and different it was to see the actual orchestra playing such and such a piece, instead of just listening to it on a record, you know, and 'so and so is a particular favourite of mine', and - oh heck, she could hardly bear to even think about it.

Mr. Post his name was – Joseph Post. Before each piece of music he'd explained what the background story was and how each instrument would come in, and the sort of effect that would contribute to the overall sound of the music, and how they were meant to feel. How music 'influenced the emotions of the audience.' The only emotions *she* felt after each piece were terror and then more terror. By the time it came to stand up, she was even more worried about tripping up the steps and falling flat on her face than forgetting her speech.

'Thank you. We all enjoyed it very much,' she said.

Well at least she hoped they did. She felt like one of The Miserables.

And she'd forgotten to curtsey.

Part Three

Reflections

"It is so small a thing

To have enjoyed the sun ..."

Matthew Arnold, 'Empedocles on Etna'

McClaren's Ridge, September 1956

MARGARET

TOM SAW IT first. Or sensed it. She'd got part way through pegging out the washing. It was just the two of them; the girls at school, Rob gone to Morrisbrook till late for a Field Day.

No hurry. It doesn't actually hurt to reach up now, but she finds she is still moving cautiously. Rob put everything through the wringer before he went – doesn't want her to exert herself.

'Mum!' Tom's voice is high and urgent, almost a whisper. He is staring at something in the grass near the shade of the mangoes.

'Mum!' At first she thinks one of the girls has left a skipping rope out. Then she stiffens – a snake? God, that's all she needs, all the men away – no, it's too thin, not quite the right colour or texture. Tom is being unusually cautious, but he has dragged his blanket closer across the yard, and is pointing a chubby finger towards a grey line, drawn further out now from the deep shadow, through dappled green and onto the open lawn.

'Don't touch it Tom,' she puts the clothes basket down and moves over to him. Although her first inclination is to scoop him up and away, he seems to have some innate sense that while it isn't just a skipping rope, maybe it's not quite as scary as a snake – but whatever it is does command respect.

'Oh look,' she is delighted, almost feels like applauding. She has seen this once or twice before, but never so many. 'It's caterpillars, Tom,' she says. And it is; an endless crawling lifeline of hairy caterpillars, linked, end-to-end, heading blindly out into the sunlight.

He is entranced. 'Ca'pillas,' he smiles up at her then settles on his haunches to study the progress of the furry conga line. She sits down with him. Watching.

'Where go?'

'They're moving somewhere, sweetie. Maybe to find another home. I guess that's how they stay safe. Other animals might think they're a snake.'

'Train,' he says.

'It is,' she says, 'it's just like a train. Clever boy.'

That was the first thing Rob said. 'Go down to Sydney love, get a sleeper. We'll be right.' But she doesn't want to. Not this time, anyway. They'd be sympathetic, but she doesn't want sympathy. She doesn't want to see or talk to anyone.

She'd like to be able to wind herself into a cocoon. She wants to be here with Tom, on the lawn, watching caterpillars in the sun and still be pregnant; or to have not been pregnant at all.

The line is extending inexorably across the yard. Slow, purposeful, dead ahead, forward movement achieved by minute ripples that move right along its length like an electrical impulse. Hundreds, it seems. Still emerging from the leaf litter beneath the mangoes and soldiering bravely over the open terrain – to where, she wonders. Leaving home. When they've settled in to where they are going, will they become moths, butterflies? Will they be allowed to live?

She hadn't wanted to see but she knew. It would have been a boy. The bloody tomatoes. She should have stopped. She'd known from about four months that it wasn't right. The cramps. Bleeding. The bloody farm. Rob feels guilty. She feels guilty. Why? The caterpillars are still coming – how far back does it go – the line, the guilt, the blood – so much blood, and the nurses, hanging out the window in the corridor to see the Olympic torch bearers running past in the street below, all the crowds clapping and cheering, car horns blaring, whistles blowing, marching bands, and there she was doubled up and bleeding all over the crisp white hospital sheets, calling out and no one to hear. Oh, they did feel terrible, but there wasn't much they could have done. It was pretty much all over in a few minutes. But such pain. And then just the emptiness. And life has to go on, doesn't it.

The silence is absolute. The caterpillars are now a furred gray line dividing the lawn in half from top to bottom. She remembers having read somewhere that butterflies only live for five days. Can this be true? It seems a cruel fate for such a careful, full day's journey towards the next stage of life.

Tom has barely moved. Once or twice he has run to the shade of the mangoes on tiptoe so as not disturb their progress, and then toddled along beside the line as far as the toilet and the bushes that mark the waste ground and the compost heap behind, where their trail disappears. Then he returns to continue his vigil, still mesmerized and obviously satisfied that they pose no threat to him or his blanket.

She has stopped worrying that he might try to touch them; sorry Rob and the girls could not be here. He would know what these are.

Not until the last of the caterpillars wriggles out of view does she suddenly become aware of a tractor in the distance, the chatter of birds, the humming of late morning insects. A light breeze has picked up, stirring the few pieces of clothing she did peg out, seemingly half a day ago.

'Ca'pillas gone?' says Tom, bottom lip about to quiver.

'I think they might have gone to get some lunch, sweetie,' she rises, 'and I think it's time for yours too. Then a little sleep, and what a story we've got for Daddy, eh?'

The washing can wait till after she's put him down – this is not the time of daily afternoon storms.

She's actually hungry too. And looking forward to Rob coming home.

McClaren's Ridge, Winter 1963

CATHY

I HAD A bit of a sore throat yesterday.

'How do you feel this morning,' Mum looks in before breakfast.

Well, I had a salt gargle and a spoonful of honey before bed, but it was one of those nights when your legs start to ache and when you wake up your head feels a bit heavy – I mean, I could get out of bed if I really wanted to, but it's a bit cool this morning and there's nothing much happening at school.

Mum says I probably caught a chill by not wearing something on my feet up at Mount Tamborine. She's making vegetable soup, so we can have some for lunch. Lots of vegetables, sometimes rice and a spoonful of Bonox for extra flavour, with hot buttered toast. In the warmer weather it would probably be Saos with avocado or Vegemite. Those sorts of lunches are one of the best things about staying home sick. I'll rug up on the couch with a blanket and we can watch the midday movie.

I just like being able to sleep in and stay warm and read. We're studying *Lorna Doone* and *Lord of the Flies*, so I can get the flies read in the morning, and then start on *Lorna Doone* again. It'll be my second time for both, but sometimes that's even better. The sad and beautiful things and the scary things are even sadder and scarier than the first time, because you know they're coming and you can start to worry about them sooner. And because you know everyone better – Ralph and Piggy, Jon Ridd, Carver Doone, things matter more.

Mum gets heaps of books from The Book Club and The School of Arts library too, and she gives me the good ones to read. If they make a film as well that's always good too. I'm still not sure which is better to do first, but when they both just make you live in a different world for a while, like *East of Eden* or *Intruder in the Dust*, it's terrific.

Most of the kids in my class go to the pictures on Saturday night now. I've done that a few times when I stayed with Christine or one of the others. Ages ago too, when I was friends with two of the bean pickers' girls, they said we're going to the pictures tonight, would Cathy like to come and stay the weekend. Mrs. Collins looked in the paper and said here's one that sounds as if it would be good for the girls – *Baby Doll*. Mum said Oh my god when I said that's what we'd seen, but then she thought it was funny. I thought it was one of the best pictures I ever saw, and always since then, it's been the ones like that I remember most – *The Long Hot Summer, A Streetcar Named Desire, Suddenly Last Summer* –sultry women and mean, moody men, the steamy weather. You can feel the heat, smell the perspiration and the all that simmering emotion under the genteel veneer. Or *Splendour in the Grass*. That's how I want to feel. Doomed young love.

Living out here I don't get much chance to experience that sort of life. Kids at school (even boys I like) will sometimes ask will I be at the pictures next Saturday night, and I hint that I might be, when all the time I know that if I go to the pictures on Saturday I'll be having lunch on the banks of the Saltwater Channel and looking after Tom when Dad's dropped us off. Waiting till the Matinee starts. Usually we'll get a pie and a milkshake, and if the bakery has any cream horns left before they close we get one of them instead an ice cream later. At least it's a chance to get into a nice dress, hairy legs or not. Well, they're not hairy now, but Mum still hasn't noticed.

I said to her ages ago, everyone else in the class shaves their legs, it's bad enough having legs that are not very tan without them being hairy into the bargain. She said you're mad, once you do it, you'll have to keep doing it forever. They'll just grow back thicker and darker. I don't care I said, it would be worth not having the embarrassment, and I finally did it anyway in the shower the other night with Dad's razor and shaving cream. So that's a bit better, even though I still haven't got any nice court shoes and my best winter dress really needs to be a bit shorter. There's nothing much I can do about not having blue eyes, or green which would be even better. Mine are not even a colour that is anything else – hazel, it sounds like an old lady or something.

What I should be doing on a Saturday is going to ballet class, but back when I was the right age to start was when the Ford ran down the hill into the gully. For a while we could only get lifts into Kalinga with Harry, let alone all the way to Booralla, which was the closest place for ballet lessons. I used to get ballet stories and books about Pavlova all the time for Christmas though, and I'd watch my feet in the reflection of the glass door of the bookcase to practice the positions. So I always sit straight and if I'm in the queue at the pictures or waiting for groceries, I'll stand in the third position so people will think how graceful, she must learn ballet. Well anyway, I do get to go to the pictures, which I love.

Mum does too, so we look forward to the old lunchtime ones on TV. It's always someone like Joan Crawford or Barbara Stanwyk getting all fierce and evil with Joseph Cotton or Dana Andrews with wide trousers and wavy hair. I don't know what Joan Crawford was thinking with that lipstick. I saw a picture of her once before she started wearing that sort of makeup and she was beautiful. Looked a bit like Mum in a photo we've got of her and aunty Carmel, all dressed up in suits and rolled hair before they got married. Then you get people like Stanley Baker, or Richard Widmark being a hopeless person on the run, who hasn't really done anything except be angry, but he's forced into a life of crime and has no friends. There's usually not much choice but for them to get shot in the end.

So the boys have gone to school and Dad's at work, and I stay in bed reading while Mum tidies up a bit. Maybe some washing with the new improved twin-tub semi-automatic, or running over the lounge room rug with the new improved carpet sweeper. We have more mod cons these days. Then she puts the vegetables in the pressure cooker so they can cook slowly all morning and the whole house gets that cosy and safe at home smell of winter soup, and when it gets a bit warmer, I put my slippers on and sit on the front verandah in the sun.

It's *Brief Encounter* today. The Midday Movie. That's the other sort – stiff upper lips and tragedy in the lives of ordinary and not very beautiful people. Trevor Howard's all right though. Better than wet old Leslie Howard trying to be Ashley Wilkes in *Gone with the Wind*. What a letdown that was.

By the time it's finished it's two o'clock, so I lie on the couch a bit longer, get over feeling sad and finish *Lord of the Flies*, but instead of going back to *Lorna Doone* I start *A Summer Place*, which Mum has just finished and says I'll like. I love it - I'm about half way through by teatime. I know I like things neat and tidy, but kill me if I ever end up like Ken Jorgenson's mother-in-law in that book. She just fell off the ladder trying to get the vacuum cleaner to a part of the picture rail that no one's ever going to see. I'll try and finish it after tea, but I'm getting up now because I'll go to school tomorrow.

There's a double geography. We're getting ready for a Marine Biology excursion where we'll be staying away at Lennox Head camp for two days, and I don't want to miss Latin either. Who can relax anyway with Tom and Nicky fighting about something senseless like whether or not Fred Trueman will get more wickets than Richie Benaud in the Ashes Test next summer. I've already promised to take Tom to the Brisbane match and he's counting the days, even though it's months away. Nicky is really still too little to have any idea, except to disagree with whatever Tom says, but when I say 'What about Wes Hall?' they both give me pitying looks.

My throat feels all right. It's just nice to stay home with Mum once in a while.

The Brisbane Limited, September 1963

TOM

HIS FATHER DROVE them to Booralla to catch the 3.35pm train. That was just a normal passenger train, but when they got to Morrisbrook, they changed trains and boarded the sleeping berth train that had started in Brisbane. They had tickets booked so that when they found their carriage, other people weren't sitting in their numbers. They will arrive at Central Station, which is the closest one to Grandma's, at 8.34 am.

He likes to study the timetable. He knows the names of all the towns they will go through, even though it will be dark for a lot of the time, and The Brisbane Limited is an Express, so they will only stop at the main stations. Because they'll be on the train right through the night. Like a moving hotel.

It was 7.25 pm when they boarded at Morrisbrook, so once they had found their carriage and put their luggage in, they went down to the Dining Car to have some tea. Their seats had just looked like ordinary seats then, with the luggage racks up above. But after they got back, the guard had fixed up all the seats so that they were sleeping bunks. The top bunks don't have rails though, like the ones in the Rocky Point house, only straps that hook up to the wall, so Mum and Nicholas got the ones on the bottom. The sheets are very white and stiff and the blankets all have NSWGR on them for New South Wales Government Railways.

Everything on the tables in the Dining Car was rattling in time with the wheels on the tracks. Mum was a bit worried all the time that they'd spill their milk, or the plates would slide off into their laps, but it was smooth moving, not jumpy, and Air-Conditioned. She let them order their own things off the menu. He was playing a game with Nicholas about who could get their feet out of the way first, but as usual, Nicholas had to start whining and being a chicken, so Mum said 'What's going on?'

'Tom keeps kicking me under the table.'

'Leave him alone,' she said, 'I'm not going all the way to Sydney with you two bickering, so just cut it out. And I'll say this once, and I won't say it again. I want you on your best behaviour while we're down there. Grandma will be really busy with all of us there, and if there's any trouble, you'll be sorry when we get home.'

'What about Cathy,' he said. Mum told him not to be ridiculous, Nicholas laughed, and Cathy just smiled and raised her eyebrows like she always does.

They all took turns to have a wash in the little shiny sink that that came down from the wall in the toilet section which was in a corner of the cabin and so small it all fitted in behind a cupboard door with little towels and soaps that had railway stamps on them.

You couldn't tell how fast the train was going, except once in a while, when they went past a town that was too small to stop in, the lights flashed by so quickly he knew they must be really speeding along, and he had to count faster in his head to keep time with the hum and clack of the wheels. It was a bit hard on the bunk, and he wondered if they would ever get properly to sleep, moving like that, and with the noise, but once Mum pulled the blinds down and he lay in bed rocking with the train, it felt like it does when a band plays and you march in time without thinking about it, or when he had the anaesthetic to have his knee sown up after he tripped and fell on the old fence post that was buried in the long grass and the doctor told him to count backwards.

He knew he must have gone to sleep, but he couldn't remember when. And now he felt the rocking again, and he could just make out the pictures, those photographs of famous places in New South Wales, like The Three Sisters and Jenolan Caves and Bondi Beach, just below where the wall curved into the ceiling above his head. The carriage was a bit lighter, even though the blinds were still down on the windows, and the others were starting to move around and sit up. He reached down and pulled the blind back a bit to see outside. Everything looked pink and grey with only a few housetops and dark trees showing above the mist.

Mum said 'Come on, we want to be dressed and ready in plenty of time when we get to the Station,' and he remembered him and Nicholas getting new haircuts, and everything new to wear.

Long socks, V-necked jumpers with ribs because it might be cold in Sydney in September, serge shorts and new shoes. Mostly grey, and a bit bigger, so they can still grow into them and they will be good for school later. He's got a blue stripe on his socks and on his jumper, and Nicholas has red. And Cathy will be a bridesmaid. Susan is getting married to Ross in Sydney and they are all going to the wedding, and Dad will come down too, on the weekend, so they can all drive back together.

Except Susan, because she will be going to live somewhere else now, with Ross.

Sydney, September 1963

CATHY

SUSAN TOLD ME the Distrix story today. When we were under the hair dryers. Well, it was Gran's story really – land, families, a doomed love affair. It was a bit like hearing a fairy story when you thought about how Gran and Mrs. Robinson are now, but they were Maisie Simpson and Iris McClaren then and they were best friends at school. And they did have tennis parties down at Acacia Flats, and Gran *was* a really good player.

Susan said Gran showed her a photo one day. One of those lovely old sepia pictures, with of all of them in tennis skirts down to their knees and white shoes, lined up under the jacarandas. Except for the tennis racquets in their hands, she said they looked as if they were all off to a croquet afternoon. Iris was standing next to Wal – she looked beautiful Susan said, and Wal was really tall and handsome. Tiny Maisie, with her hair done up in ribbons, was next to them, with Duncan, who was Wal's younger brother, on the end. And Susan said Gran, that was Maisie, is looking straight at the camera, but Duncan's looking down at her, and if you ever saw anyone in love, that was it. Susan said Gran told her it was always a bit complicated, because Iris really liked Duncan too, but Wal asked her out first. Then Wal and Duncan went to the War, and after about a year, Duncan was reported missing.

So Iris finally said yes to Wal and moved onto McClaren's Ridge. Then, when the War was nearly over, Duncan came back. But he never was the same, Gran said – shell-shock they called it – and in and out of hospitals with infections that kept flaring up. And by that

75

time she'd married Old Pa – well, he was only young then and his name was Charlie. Charlie Lovett. So that was the end of her being friends with Iris as far as Wal Robinson was concerned. And definitely the end of Maisie and Duncan. I went to visit him once or twice at the hospital, Gran said to Susan ... I was so sad that I never waited for him. I wanted to look after him – but I had a home by then, she said, I already had a husband and I had the babies.

And home was on the Lovett's side of the valley.

The Lovetts and the McClarens had been arguing over land boundaries for so long that most of the relatives still alive didn't even know what it was all about. (Except that Susan thinks the land our house ended up being on was one of the parcels of land whose ownership they'd never sorted out.) And Wal was never one to forgive anyone for anything. He blamed everyone who wasn't a McClaren for what had happened to Duncan, and anyone who was a Lovett. True love and friendship didn't come into it.

'Gran looked so sad when she was talking about Duncan,' Susan said, 'and about Iris. I couldn't believe that about Wal when she first told me. Fancy making so many people's lives unhappy like that. And for nothing really. Gran hardly cared about that part of it any more. I mean I'd be furious, but she mainly felt sad for Iris. And about Duncan of course. He died in his early thirties, she said, from flu. And he didn't ever marry anybody else.'

By that time the hairdresser had started shooting Gossamer Net all over our stupid hairdos, even though I said I didn't want any, and we had to keep our mouths closed, but I wondered if Susan ever thought about when she was little. I suddenly felt awful remembering all my stupid jokes about wicked stepsisters and things. But I wouldn't have made jokes about it if I thought she would be upset. She was always my older sister and mum was our mother. Maybe I'm old enough now to ask how she really felt about it all, but now she's too busy with Ross and the wedding and all that, and they'll be going away tonight. You just don't think about these things.

I said to Mum, 'How old was Susan when you married Dad?'

'She was nearly ready to start school.'

'So you had a ready-made family.'

And then Mum got too busy as well.

Sydney, 1963

MARGARET

SHE THINKS OF hers and Rob's Day.

Like a business meeting or an interview in comparison. Just after the War it was, and he was divorced, so a Catholic wedding was out of the question. Not that she practiced anyway. And she had no desire whatsoever to put her children through the Catholic school experience of her own childhood. And his High Anglican father wasn't interested in any contact, let alone the shame of a second wedding. Rob already seemed to be the unofficial family black sheep. A Registry Office with the minimum required number of witnesses was the only real choice.

And through all this, Susan, a remote and troubled little soul, who had already turned five and still didn't even know Rob very well, stayed with the wonderful Mrs. Clancy, who'd been a foster mother to her in the two or three years since his first wife, Susan's own mother, had chosen to follow her heart in another direction while Rob was away. Doing his bit to keep the country safe.

And here is Susan, grown up, looking radiant, as they say in the social pages – but she really does – smiling and happy and obviously loved by all the Whitworths. She recalls Susan's early misgivings, as the arrangements seemed to grow more and more elaborate and the guest list swelled – it was one of those *if we ask Uncle Peter, we can't not invite Richard and Nancy* situations - and *how long is it since I set foot in a church – if ever – I'll feel like a hypocrite.* But it's all gone like clockwork – it even stopped raining when the cars arrived outside the church – and everyone is dancing and eating and enjoying themselves. Rob is proud and Cathy cried, and the boys behaved.

She herself is a little overwhelmed by all the Whitworths. Not that all of them are anything other than pleasant and chatty, unfailingly polite and apparently genuinely interested in life in the north; but she can't help feeling that a small crop farm in McClaren's Ridge doesn't really present anything much to compare with the glamour of cattle stations, beach houses and B. & S. Balls. Which doesn't stop her from admitting to herself that she is not prepared to hear anyone else cast aspersions.

What she can't help reflecting on is how quickly time has passed, how far they have come in some ways, she and Rob, but how much of a struggle it has been, and no indications that the future will be any easier. But she is beginning to realise, on what have become more infrequent trips back to the city, that she actually prefers to be in McClaren's Ridge.

SUMMER FEET

Part Four

Rivers crossed

"Things do not change, we change."

Henry David Thoreau, 'Walden'

McClaren's Ridge, November 1958

CATHY

NICKY'S ON TO little tins of rice custard and Heinz brains and things now, which must be horrible but he seems to like them. Susan and I always want to feed him, but he likes Mum to do it best. A lot of the time if we all hang around, Mum says it just distracts him, but I thought he might like a song. Then Susan said stop teasing Tom, and I said I'm not. She said you are – Mum, she keeps asking him if he wants to hear *The Teddy Bears' Picnic*, and I said well it is his favourite song and Susan said you know it always makes him cry now. I said I don't know why, she said you do so.

Well, all right, but he looks so cute when his mouth goes all square, and we can stop before we get to the last verse. He still likes the rest of it. It's the same with the Enchanted Forest chapter of *Winnie the Pooh*. That makes me cry too, but I always wanted to hear it. Anyway, he's so embarrassing it's not funny. Right in the middle of the post office the other day we were, and he said to Mum in this loud voice that everyone in Kalinga must've heard to hurry up because Nick's doing grunties in his nappy.

There were people's mothers there.

And Susan's getting a bit stupid. All she cares about is boys – well one boy. She doesn't draw horses on her exercise books any-more – just pictures of surfers all over the place. She got mad at me the other day because I said something about being in love with Danny Johnson, which she is, and Mum heard us.

Danny Johnson, she said, Joyce and Shorty's boy? He always used to win everything in sight at the Swimming Carnivals didn't he? And I said he's one of the Surfwall Boys. Mum said what's a Surfwall boy and Susan said nothing, it's just what they call the surf club boys. But later on she said she'd kill me if I talked about him anymore.

Anyway, he is. He's the main one, because his Dad runs the Headland Pool at South Beach. Well, there are three pools – the shallow one for littlies, the big one with a diving board and lanes that they use for racing and carnivals, and the middle one where they have lessons and bronze training and stuff. And that pool's out on the edge of the headland in the sea rocks. Sometimes if we have big storms they have to close it because the waves come right up over the wall.

So everyone calls it the Surfwall Pool. And that's why Danny and his mates are called the Surfwall Boys. They have these competitions whenever Shorty's away. Or kids reckon sometimes Danny even sneaks them in at night. They climb over the surfwall and they have to see who can hang out over the rocks the longest without getting wiped out.

Mum doesn't know the half of it. But I'm not going to be the one who says anything. At least not while Susan's around.

December 1957

SUSAN

WELL, THEY WERE finally moving out of the Stone Age in McClaren's Ridge. Or should that be the Ice Age. Or the Kerosene Age. Anyway, electricity was actually getting put on next year. Just as she was about to leave of course.

She and Cathy would often have a sort of *Pick-a-Box* quiz when they were coming home from school, so the walk up the hill didn't seem so long, and Susan had asked her to name three things she thought would be good about getting electricity. Cathy couldn't think of anything at first except switching the lights on and off. Heavens, Susan could think of a million things, but then, Cathy couldn't really remember Melbourne.

Just imagine having a proper refrigerator and bed lamps. Dad had already bought fluorescent tubes for the kitchen, and nice round flat lights for the walls in the lounge room. She couldn't think why they were called "oysters" – she'd never seen anything that looked less like an oyster in her life. But she couldn't wait. And neither could Mum. It might even mean they'd get a television set, but it was a pretty safe bet that Dad wouldn't want one. Gran said she was going to have one as soon as she could get Pa to buy it, but he didn't really like the sound of electricity. He thought they wouldn't be allowed to use it after six o'clock. He had this idea that everything would get turned off then or something. That's what he told Gran anyway.

When Susan told Mum, she said 'That'd be Old Pa – another one of his mad ideas. You use it when you want to, not when they tell you, unless there's a blackout or rations. He's probably getting confused with what happened during the war. Still,' she said, 'there'll never be anyone who can grow sweet peas like he does.'

Tom was excited about it too. He didn't know exactly what it was, but everyone was talking about it, so he never stopped asking questions about the "lectriclines". Partly because there might be heavy machinery coming to get things done. Dad had made him a sandpit, and he spent hours moving sand from one end of it to the other with his Tonka front-end loader. He was crazy about the tractor too.

He always wanted to know how things were put together and how they worked, and who made the first one. He was mad about stuff like that, and how many beans there were in a bag, even though he hadn't even started school yet. They weren't going to know what to do with him. 'Ask your father' was what people usually said, and Dad could usually tell him – even though some-times he took a very long time to explain things, because he wanted you to understand properly. Tom followed him round like a shadow – a little chatterbox shadow, sponging up facts and figures. Smiley, the pickers called him.

But once you started school, teachers were supposed to be the ones who could tell you. *Well, good luck,* Susan thought. And then, *don't get too smart; it won't be long before I'm one of them.*

April 1959

CATHY

AT LEAST NOW I've got a nice dress to wear out even if it did used to be Susan's. Puffed sleeves and a sash, blue checked with white lace around the collar. Gloves too, and a hat as well – white boater with a blue velvet ribbon, but someone will have to die or get married before I wear that again. Probably a bit bright for a funeral, but everyone gets dressed up properly to go shopping in Hartley, so I hope it's not too long before we go there again. Mum and I went over with Dad for a Field Day last year, but I felt awful because we must have been about the only people there without hats and gloves.

I really liked some of the hymns at Sunday School and the *Common Prayer Book*. Can I get one for my birthday I said, so Mum and Dad gave me a lovely one with a mother of pearl cover. Most of the lessons were the same as what we have in Scripture – the loaves and fishes, the road to Damascus, the Lord throwing the sinners out of the temple and everything – but they're all good stories. We've got a huge *Readers' Bible* at home and whenever Mum's run out of books to read she picks a section out of that to read again. The Creed is nice and some of the psalms, especially the valley of the shadow of death, and after my first couple of times at Sunday School I organized for us to say Grace at home before tea, which Rev. Peterson says we all should do to give thanks for being so much better off than the starving Armenians and so on.

But it's all too difficult, so I might as well get more interested in butterflies.

At the start of the year, Rev Peterson came to give all of us who would be turning eleven this year a special talk. All about the glory of John the Baptist and how we are all washed in the blood of the lamb and how baptism is our key to the Christian life, but that now we are on the brink of our adult life it is time to make our own commitment.

'I don't know if I can come to Confirmation classes,' I said to Christine, after the first two talks. 'There aren't too many days I can stay late after school, or get Dad to pick me up.'

'But you have to come to classes,' she said, 'or you can't get confirmed. Diane's Mum's making her dress, but I'm allowed to pick one out to buy next time we go over to Hartley. Have you got yours yet?'

'Mum's taking me down to Booralla on Saturday morning to have a look in Patterson's,' I said. Patterson's Haberdashery and Drapery. And we were going, but Confirmation dresses weren't on the list.

A new dress, on top of the hat, the gloves and the prayer book. Dad would probably start talking about ships coming in. And I'd have to be able to stay in town at least one afternoon a week, for lessons and practice. I wasn't too sure about eating the body and drinking the blood of our Lord anyway.

But I couldn't just sit in the pew looking really interested in the floral arrangements, or actually act deaf and dumb, while everyone else went up get the Sacrament. The plate would probably come rattling past a few more times, and I only had one sixpence to put in each week. I still don't know what those little packages were – some of the older ladies especially, put little lavender scented balled-up hankies in the plate sometimes. Maybe they'd been saving threepences for a month of Sundays, or was it some other token of faith they were offering – dried pansies, logan berries, rosellas or something. I could never ask without seeming sinfully curious, so I'll never know now.

It was the first lesson when they told us what would happen at the ceremony and gave us a timetable for practice in the Catechism and everything. Denise's Hunt's mother was going to be taking some of the afternoon classes, so she addressed us about the sort of outfits we would be wearing and asked us to think about how to conduct ourselves and the particular gifts we might be able to use in the Christian life.

'This will be one of the most important days of your young life in the Church,' she said. 'Between baptism and marriage, this will be the next step in your growth as a committed Christian.'

I was already getting sweaty palms.

Then the Rev. Peterson strode in – well, if you can imagine a block of wood coming to life and striding. Or the Little Tin Soldier in our Hans Andersen Fairy Tales, with a very loud voice and stiff black hair that would not lie down for Brylcreem or the Lord.

'Boys and girls,' he said … there was only one boy in the class and that was Rev. Peterson's son, Lewis, who also had difficult hair and very thick glasses. The girls were nearly all from Kalinga Primary, my Scripture class, with some from the high school and one or two from Pelican Point, and nearly all their mothers and fathers went to church as well … . 'Boys and girls, you were baptised into the Lord's care at birth,' my sense of joy got a bit smaller, 'this has been your shelter … now, on the eve of adulthood, you have the chance to affirm that commitment yourself, to renew the baptismal promises made by your parent and godparents. You are able to move closer to the worship of the lord, and you will be able to partake of the body and blood …'

No one else seemed to be worried.

'This then, is the next step on the road to accepting the responsibilities of life as an adult Christian, being god's servants and increasing in Holy Spirit, securing your place in the everlasting kingdom, your passport to celebrating the sanctity of the marriage vows in his holy dwelling, and being one ...'

The Bishop would be also blessing us with his presence and the following week we could set out on the road to our Gospel challenge. I started to think about ways to explain why I couldn't come to any more confirmation classes.

It was raining on the Tuesday after that, so I had to catch the bus. I did go to Sunday School, and I went to confirmation, but things had got to where I would never be able to join the saved. Rev. Peterson went through the order of service and the dialogue we would have with the Bishop. I could deny all rebellion against god and be called out of the darkness into His marvellous light, but it doesn't matter. I failed the first question.

"Have you been baptised in the name of the Father, the Son and the Holy Ghost?" Well, no, I haven't.

I'd be quite happy to stand in a shallow creek somewhere or whatever people do if they missed out as babies and they're too big to be held over the font. But it's too late. If Lewis Peterson wasn't such a creep I could get him to ask his dad what people do, but I sure as heck can't tell Rev Petersen, and all the others would think it's just plain weird not to even be christened.

Anyway, I'd rather go walking in the rainforest looking for scenery and butterflies. And have picnics. That's what Dad likes to do on Sundays now that we've got a car again and they don't have to work on the farm all the time.

We all go on Sunday drives. Well we used to. I bet next time we go Susan will be staying with Yvonne or Barbara in town so they can hang around the beach or Johnson's pool.

Dad's got exercise books for all of us so we can list all the butterflies we see, and then we look them up in the butterfly book to find out their proper names and we draw pictures of them. Mine's nice and neat and I like drawing, but Dad's and Susan's are always coloured in so perfectly they look like pictures out of a nature book.

Tom hasn't got much in his book yet. He likes to run off miles ahead of everyone so he can find things first, but Dad has to keep telling him if he doesn't slow down and be quiet he'll scare everything away and then Tom gets cranky and doesn't want to look for anything. And then they both get cranky. Mum reckons she can't draw, but she still does them because Dad says anyone can draw if they try and she likes going for walks and finding out about them too. We see lots of Blue Triangles and Golden Wanderers but we really want to see a Birdwing. We have planted some special vines to attract the caterpillars for that butterfly and some are nearly ready. Lovely bright green cocoons.

I think I'm damned anyway.

You're allowed to go on a plane by yourself when you're ten, so last year I went to Sydney on TAA to stay at Grandma's for a week. The hostesses looked after me, and Uncle Mick came to the airport to pick me up and take me to their house in Ashgrove. Where Mum used to live.

The last time I was there was when we went down after the cyclone when Tom was little, but I still remembered it: the front gate that always creaks, with the curly lace wire, the black and white checked tiles on the path up to the front door that made you feel as though you were walking on a chessboard. Flower patterns on the ceiling that you can look at when you're in bed and the emerald green and ruby red panes of glass in the front windows that put magic light in the front rooms late in the afternoon. A big picture in Grandma's bedroom too, of Jesus with long curly hair and a little lamp burning where his heart would be.

They got bread delivered by the baker on a cart with a draught horse, bottles of milk came round, and you could just walk up to the shop on the corner to buy ice creams. Grandma already had a television set, so I watched the *Mickey Mouse Club* every afternoon. People say Annette's the nicest, but I liked Darlene and Cheryl better.

Most days I played with Pauline and Carol Byrnes next door. They have nuns for teachers like mum did when she went to school. Just about everyone in Parry Street is Catholic. I went to Mass with the family and it was lovely in the church, and Novena is good too. They'd been learning about the power of prayer, and because Pauline said one day that it wasn't fair that boys could stand up to wee and girls have to sit down, Carol said well if we all prayed hard enough every day, together and also in bed at night, then our bodies might get changed.

Well, I think God must have put that in the too hard basket. We all prayed really hard for four days, and checked ourselves first thing every morning, but nothing happened. Carol said He must have other plans for us or it was just the wrong time and He was too busy, but Pauline said it might have been because of me. Not being Catholic and destined for purgatory and everything. It's not your fault, she said, but Proddies can never really be saved.

So Confirmation mightn't make any difference. I was getting sick of Sunday school anyway. If I ever need to get married, maybe I'll see about it then.

At least I've got some good shoes to wear to the pictures now.

Mount Tamborine, Easter 1963

TOM

THEY'RE NOT SUPPOSED to be out here. He wishes they weren't now, because it's almost dark in this part of the rainforest. Only a black pattern of leaves way up high, and long, skinny beams of sunlight like someone's shining a torch through the trees. He'd been hoping it might be time to go back, but it's only half past two. He's glad Melvin's got his waterproof watch and Swiss army knife.

Maybe he should have minded his own business. Cathy and Melvin tried to sneak off without him after lunch, but he made them take him. Said he'd tell where they were going if they didn't. Cathy wanted to show Melvin the old part of the lodge where they stayed when she was little and there was only her and Susan and Mum and Dad. Little huts that look like storage sheds now. And a secret path she remembered.

He'd caught them whispering about it last night. Cathy was saying that no one is allowed to use it anymore because it might be dangerous, but it was the one that lead to the Wishing Tree. He heard Melvin say that it sounded like a really good adventure. He could probably do some good exploring with Melvin if it was just the two of them, but Cathy and Melvin always have to both go. They always have secrets. When *he* asked Cathy what tree did she say, she wrinkled up her nose at him and called him Big Ears.

He could even explore and discover things on his own if he could ever get away without Nicholas spoiling everything. But that usually happens and then he can't do anything exciting. An expedition to the Secret Wishing Tree definitely has to be better than running around with a butterfly net or listening for bird calls and having to walk everywhere so quietly in case you scare them off. He just wishes all the vines weren't called things like wait-a-while and burny and blood and strangler.

People once found a crashed aeroplane way down in one of the valleys. They had to hack their way through places no one had ever discovered before. There probably weren't any more of those, but if he found something that might be poisonous, strange toadstools or something that even people like Joseph Banks never knew about, he'd be famous. There might be some inside the tree. It was hollow. That was what made it so special Cathy said. It was one of those huge fig trees that had started growing in the hollow of another rainforest tree where the branch meets the main trunk. The fork. Then all its roots grew down to meet the ground and once they started spreading and the second tree just got bigger and stronger, the old tree just rotted away underneath. The ranger had told them how the birds did that, by carrying seeds around up above the rainforest canopy and then dropping them in different places to start new trees. That's why they call them strangler figs. But what you got after hundreds of years looked like a big church door or a cave.

So it would look like the big old tree in the historical photos in the Common Room of people like Gran Lovett's wedding pictures. In those days they came up to the mountains in horses and buggies for camps and picnics. He wonders if they walked out at night to see the glow-worms like little blue stars on the clay bank at Deadman's Creek, or sang *Click Go the Shears* and *The Wild Colonial Boy* around the fire after dinner. Before the slide show last night, he went in to have another look. In one picture, some ladies in hats and long dresses were standing inside a tree and it looked pretty famous, but it could be a different one. Except that there was a card pinned to the wall under the photo saying that the track to this Venerable Tree is no longer Accessible.

He looked 'accessible' and 'venerable' up in the dictionary. They've got a little library next to the Common Room where they keep all the old books that guests have signed and encyclopedias about the flora and fauna of Australia and South East Queensland. Some of the things the old guests said were a bit corny, but it's interesting to see how long ago they came. Maybe he can discover an accessible track to the venerable tree. That might be better than a poisonous discovery because he'd have to test that out.

At least then someone might be pleased or surprised by something he's done and not just say 'that's good' and be really thinking that he should win races or come top in spelling all the time anyway. Like when he found out how to make rotten egg gas with Cathy's chemistry set by himself. No one thought that was good. And nearly every time he gets into trouble it's because of something stupid Nicholas made him do.

But he's beginning to wish he didn't make Cathy and Melvin let him come with them. Maybe he can come back one day and find a different track. One that hasn't got big old tree roots like skeleton's fingers reaching up out of the ground through the dead leaves. Where you can't hear those catbirds the ranger told them about that sound like babies screaming. Not one where you could get lost, even with Melvin's compass, and no one would know.

They'd found the path, up behind the huts. It wasn't one that groups of people went on to get to the views or the waterfalls. They had seen some little waterfalls but there weren't any signs to say which waterfalls they were. So they mightn't even be marked on a map. There were no labels to tell you the names of the trees either, or arrows to tell you this was the right way. They might need Melvin's compass later, but it wouldn't be much use now, because Cathy wasn't even sure which way it was.

'Why do we keep going,' he said, 'it might get dark before we find the Tree. And you're going to cop it already with those wet clothes.' A bit further back they'd had to get across a little creek. Cathy was showing off to Melvin as usual, and she lost her balance on one of the slippery rocks. Now half her back was wet and all stained with moss and mud.

'Don't be such a scaredy cat. There aren't any other tracks. Anyway, by the time we get back I'll be dry and I can brush most of the dirt off.'

And stupid Melvin was agreeing with her. 'Come on,' he said. 'Even if we don't find it, we're still having an adventure.'

By the time they got to the old rope bridge though, Cathy knew where they were. That was right, she said – you had to go across that to get to the Magic Faraway Tree.

When he said 'I thought you said it was the Wishing Tree,' she just rolled her eyes at Melvin as if to say 'Little brothers!' But Melvin hasn't got any brothers or sisters anyway, so he wouldn't know.

She stayed where she was though. 'It is still a long way from here,' she said to Melvin, 'we started in the morning last time and it was way after lunch when we got back.'

'We've come this far.' Melvin wanted to go right on to the tree now they'd heard so much about it.

'I really don't think we should', she said, 'it's getting too late and I don't want us all to get into trouble.'

Oh yeah. 'Who's the scaredy cat now?' he said, stepping a bit closer to where Melvin was standing, 'You're just not game to walk over that bridge.'

'Well, maybe I'm not,' she said. 'I certainly don't want you to. It looks a lot more dangerous that it did when we came up last time. Look at all those rotten boards.'

He remembered the little rusty sign near the barbed wire they crawled through behind the huts: Track Closed. Danger: Landslides. 'Whoever heard of a landslide in a rainforest,' Melvin had said.

He looked at Melvin again and said, 'Maybe we can go one at a time. Or come back tomorrow.'

'Or I could keep going and you two wait here till I get back,' Melvin said.

That sounded like an even better idea.

'Oh, terrific,' Cathy said, 'then the rope breaks and you get stuck on the other side. Look how far down it is.' She was actually standing so far back from the edge that she couldn't see how far it was.

Finally, Melvin said 'You can see the rope is pretty frayed there,' pointing at where it was tied to the big tree on the edge. 'I might have to do some splicing before I'd trust it to hold our weight.' He unclipped the leather cover off the face of his watch to check the time, and nodded. 'Maybe we should head on back,' he said, closing the cover again, 'make our return to camp before dark.' They were staying in the lodge, but Melvin always said things like that. And he was always going to be on Cathy's side. It wasn't fair.

But it was because of Cathy that they had to go back. She was the scared one, not him.

McClaren's Ridge, December 1957

CATHY

THE BRIDGE HAS gone. It's the first thing I remember when I wake up. I try to only hear the breakfast sounds – Susan and Dad in the kitchen – but the sounds of the car and the railing are still in my head.

Ernie Lovett said, 'Surprised it didn't happen long ago. That Ruby, mad as a meat axe.' It's the last week of school, but it's still only Tuesday, and we have to go to school across the river where the bridge was. *Across those poles.*

Bits of the bridge were sinking down or falling off for ages. From inside the car, you could hear it rattle and beat like thunder and if you leaned out the window you could see water through the boards. Sometimes loose and rotten boards had to be replaced, and we had to be careful our bike wheels didn't turn sideways and go right through the cracks.

'Bloody bridge; there'll be an accident if they don't do something about it.'

That was another thing Ernie always said. Well now there is a car, all crumpled and lying at the bottom of the bank. They had to get trucks to pull it out of the water. And they've taken away the top of the bridge and the rails.

And we have to go over the river to get to school. Maybe we should fall in, then they'll take away the logs because they caused an accident too …

Dad drove us a couple of times, but it's round all the back hills then across South River on the ferry to go in on the old coach road.

Until the bridge is fixed that is. It takes ages and he really needs to be home to get the tomatoes packed before they get too ripe for the Sydney markets, and because of Mum and the baby. Anyway, I don't think he will drive us again, after me acting like I don't care about the new baby.

Because coming up the hill past the quarry after the bridge yesterday afternoon, it was really hot with the gravel and the dust and we got stones in our shoes and our socks were all red and sweaty, and my hands were slippery on the handle of my suitcase and I kept having to change arms. And Susan was walking too quickly and the mosquitoes and flies were all around our heads and legs. Even when we walked through the gully where the elephant grass almost makes a roof and the road is smooth and dark, it was still hot and the mosquitoes were worse. And there was no shade going up the last hill to home, and that's when Dad came down in the car.

He had a big smile on his face and he said 'You've got another brother – nine pounds!' and I couldn't even be bothered saying 'I could have got a new bike for ten'. He was going to the hospital, so he said Mrs. Robinson was looking after Tom and would Susan to do the tinned spaghetti for our tea, and we could all go in and see Mum and the baby tomorrow or the next day.

I was slapping at my hair, and my plaits were all coming out and I dropped my suitcase. 'These bloody mosquitoes,' I said, and then Dad drove off. Well if he'd had to walk over all those poles not looking down, and if he'd had to walk home with it still so hot and all those flies and a heavy port (I'm not supposed to say port – Mum says it's a Suitcase), well, anyway, he'd be cranky too …

But I do care about the baby. And I was hoping it would be a boy so Tom would have a playmate. Mum hasn't been very well, and the last time we thought we were getting a new baby, Mum got really sick and when just her and Dad came home from the hospital, she had to stay in bed for a while each day and they were both really quiet. Mum told us later that it was a missed carriage, and that the baby hadn't been ready. So they've been a bit worried, and Dad wouldn't let Mum help in the shed since it got hot so nothing would go wrong this time.

... but it's awful; crossing the bridge ... all through Spelling and Sums yesterday I couldn't stop thinking about it. I bet Miss Jones be surprised if she knew I didn't want school to finish at three o'clock. Well, I didn't, but it's because of those poles, and the water ...

... those big poles that are lying across the stumps that held up the bridge before the accident.

'Breakfast Cathy,' calls Dad, 'come on, you'll be late.'

'And we need to go a bit earlier because of the bridge.' That's Susan. It's all right for her; she thinks it's exciting.

We can't take our bikes across the bridge again till it's fixed ... *anyway, I don't want to ride my bike again, ever* ... we walk down our road to the mail box, then down the big road past the quarry to the river, and we catch the bus on the other side ... maybe I could be sick ...

'Come on Cathy, I won't tell you again.'

... Well, all right, then I won't have to go ... but they won't let me stay home if I'm not sick, and we're making decorations for the Christmas party at school, and I don't want to be a nuisance for Mum and Dad with the baby and everything.

So I put on my tunic and my creepy school shoes ... *smooth, slippery school shoes, slippery on those poles ...*

The poles are wide; big and grey, and they're curved, not flat on top; not like a real bridge. Even the dangerous bridge was flat on top. I think if they knew this was the only way we could get to school they'd have made more flat bits ...

If I take my shoes off I might get splinters even though the wood looks smooth, and I already have to carry my suitcase and that would be two things that would get lost if I fell in and drowned. But then I wouldn't need them would I? But if I fell in and didn't drown at least I'd still have my shoes and socks …

It's just a row of great big logs, sort of strapped on, to make the top of the bridge till it gets fixed up properly. But they're not close together. They're only on top of the long stumps that go down to the bottom of the water. With spaces in between. You can see the water in much bigger strips than you could when you looked out of the car.

And if we don't hurry we might miss the bus.

Susan says it's better to go over quickly anyway. 'Think about something else,' she says, 'and don't look down!'

So I think of sky things. About the Russian space dog up there and how many times he's been around the world now and how he'll probably have to stay in the satellite forever. And how he'd feel if he looked down …

I know it's best not to look down it makes my legs and arms go all tingly. But how can I see where my feet will land if I don't. I might tread on a place between the poles. And I don't want to look forward, because then I'll see how much further I still have to go.

Susan makes me look up. We're going home and she doesn't want me to look at the car. She's already half way across. She likes climbing trees and everything so she's okay. Yesterday she was pretending to be in the circus without a net.

In the mornings, I can think about what will happen at school, but in the afternoons, going back the other way, even though I try not to look down it's hard not to see the car. And then I think about Ruby …

That purple lipstick she used to wear that went wrinkly at the edges of her mouth. And the round spots of rouge that weren't always in the same place on both sides. And her eyelashes like clumps of wire brush. She wore big gold earrings too, a bit like the balls on our Christmas tree that made long holes in her ears. She liked to dress up for town. She always had on silver sandals and red toenail polish, and skirts with petticoats that looked as if she was going dancing, and her hair was blacker than I've ever seen anybody's.

When you walked past her outside the Pacific Hotel, you could smell talc and cigarettes – Cashmere Bouquet, mixed with Craven A's and cough-lollies. She spent a lot of time at the Pacific, when she wasn't at the Saturday matinee, or yelling at her big son, Stanley. That and driving that bloody rattletrap of his like a maniac, Ernie said, and her with no license.

She was usually about the only lady at the hotel, but she didn't go into the Bar. They've got a Lounge with red shiny couches and a fish tank, which I know about, because the first Christmas we came here and Mum couldn't cook a big proper dinner we had Christmas lunch at the Pacific. With serviette rings and bonbons and everything. Anyway, Ruby went in there, or sometimes she stood on the footpath and talked to the men through the window.

I can't do it. Maybe if people had to come and rescue us in a boat, then they'd come every day because the logs are too dangerous for kids.

'Come on you sook,' says Susan. 'You can't stay there all night. It's the only way we can get home. And the longer you stand still the worse it gets.'

Well I know that, but I feel like if I move I'll tip over …

I can't pretend about the circus; I'd be the one who has a tragic fall and gets in the newspapers.

Those trees on the other side look like the ones in the picture at home – think about Van Gogh ...

He was on at the Saturday matinee, before the accident. *Lust for Life* ... two steps forward ... and Ruby was there ... 'Don't worry, kids,' she said, that loud croaky voice and the Cashmere Bouquet going all over the canvas seats and though the dark, 'it's not real blood – they just spread tomater sauce on 'im. That's all it is – lotsa tomater sauce.' So although you knew Kirk Douglas hadn't really cut his ear off, you couldn't even pretend you nearly fainted. And Susan keeps telling people we saw "Lust for Tomato Sauce" ... which is funny, but if I laugh I might slip ... three more steps forward ...

It is like being on a high wire but I never wanted to be a trapeze artist.

I'm getting closer to where I can see the car now, but I don't want to look at that or I hear the breaking wood sounds and the screaming ...

I never talked to Ruby. Nobody told us not to but none of the kids did. She talked to everyone though, called us Love and Dearie. Some of the kids laughed at her and the men who talked to her through the window of the Pacific used to laugh about her too, when she wasn't there.

She lived just after the main houses in Acacia Flats. I used to wonder what she did when she was at home, in that house that was only just like a shed. All the walls were the same as our roof, sort of wavy tin. You couldn't imagine her and Stanley listening to the *Quiz Kids* or *Lux Radio Theatre*. There wasn't anyone else, but they had lots of cats. He worked at the Norco Factory and people said he wasn't the full quid. But it was his car ...

It's down there now. I can see it in the corner of my eye ...

I have to look at Susan, and think about trees. Or something.

'You're nearly there,' she says. 'And school's finished in a couple of days. Think about Christmas.'

That's nearly here too. But even though we've been making the decorations at school and we'll have the party on Thursday, it doesn't seem as exciting as last year. Maybe when we start waiting for Grandma's parcel to come it will seem more like Christmas.

I can almost touch Susan's hand now … just don't look at the car …

It wasn't my fault. Just the drink, they said. But I'm not riding my bike anymore, even when the bridge is fixed up. Someone else might be drunk.

'It's the drink that did it,' said Ernie. 'Bloody Ruby. Three o'clock in the afternoon and she's pissed. Sorry kids, but what can you do – shouldn't have been allowed out.'

My feet finally land on the red soil where the tow trucks scraped the grass off the bank. I can't even see the car out of the corner of my eye now. But I looked at it once. It's not really like a car anymore, just a big lump of squashed metal with a lot of the black paint scratched off. You can't imagine it ever being a smooth, shiny shape, moving along the road on wheels …

… driving over the bridge … coming towards me and my bike …

I thought it would stop because I was already on the bridge. Maybe I shouldn't have stayed there but I can't swim properly yet and I couldn't get off my bike in time and I didn't know which way to go because the car wasn't going straight. It was going really fast and crooked and I called out to Susan 'Get out of the way! Stanley's driving too fast,' but then I saw that Stanley was wearing a frilly blouse and had really black hair, and Susan did too.

'It's Ruby,' she yelled, 'she's driving his car again. Look out!' And then we both screamed and we could hear Ruby screaming and calling out to Jesus and Mary in that croaky voice and I thought I said 'She's going to crash', but no noise came out and I was even too scared to cry.

Then the rails tore with a horrible sound and made a sort of crazy gate for the car to go through; and everything was like a slow, jumpy slide show – Ruby's white face at the window, trying to get out and her mouth like blood – the car rocking on the edge of the bridge – the silver grate part at the front flashing in the sun, the shiny back tipping up, like a giant Christmas beetle waiting to dive into the river – then it flew straight down and hit the water like an explosion and we couldn't hear Ruby anymore. But it all happened really fast, and we couldn't do anything.

It took a long time to pull the car out onto the bank they said. Ruby was still in there but it was too late.

They'll be home soon, Mum and the baby. We're going to call him Nicholas because of Christmas. The big new bridge will be finished after the holidays and Dad's going to drive us round the back road for the rest of the week. Ernie will help with the packing and we won't have to walk on the poles any more.

But at least I've done one really brave, scary thing. Getting across. Because the bravest, and best thing to do, would be to see Ruby in the street and walk right up and talk to her, maybe ask about the cats. But mostly to say sorry, and I can't do that now.

McClaren's Ridge, April 1962

TOM

HE DREAMS ABOUT the soldiers on the wall. Sometimes they're like the nightmares. He's in the trenches, and he wakes up calling for someone to help him. But mostly they're brave, adventurous dreams, with him and his mates looking like the men in those big frames in Gran Lovett's lounge room, winning battles and drinking beers together in their uniforms and marching proudly with their chums, and people are waving little Union Jacks.

He likes going to Gran's after school. She's not really his grandma, it's just that there are so many Lovetts around everyone calls her Gran so people will know which Mrs. Lovett you mean.

Cathy takes him across when they go to pick up the milk after school and they're allowed to watch *Robin Hood* or *Wyatt Earp*. Cathy likes *Paladin* best, but it isn't on till 5 o'clock, and there's fires to be lit and tea to be cooked and baths to have and it gets dark by then after the May holidays. So she said to Dad 'Well if we got one, like everyone else, we could do all our jobs and still watch the really good things that come on later like *The Twilight Zone*. And the News', but he just said it was all rubbish and they couldn't afford it and the news was on the wireless anyway.

Mum usually gives them a pineapple or some bananas to take, and says don't be a nuisance, but Gran says it's all right because the littlies haven't got a television and it's a chance to put her feet up while she shells the peas or peels the potatoes. He used to pretend they were going to the Three Bears' house when he was little, be-

105

cause of the big armchairs at Gran's. Today it's a bit like *Red Riding Hood*, because Cathy's wearing her Red Cross cape that Mum made and they've got the basket. Gran's not like the wolf, but that could be Old Pa Lovett.

Cathy used to be a Red Cross Junior in primary school. When she first started, everyone had to pretend they were having accidents all the time so she could practice slings and bandages, but she's never had to do anyone properly. Dad said let's hope she doesn't have to because she fainted when they had polio needles at school and even once when she cut her finger. She's too old for the juniors now, but she's lending her uniform to one of Lovett girls for the march tomorrow.

All the Primary kids had a sort of rehearsal march this morning, up Oxley Street to the cenotaph, so the class captains could put wreaths on the memorial. The headmaster gave a speech about how Anzac Day is a day of pride and sadness for all loyal Australians, and then they marched back for a special Assembly. Terry Webster had picked up a centipede at Remembrance Park and when the choir started singing *Land of Mine* he put it on Cindy Shaw's back. It crawled right up while they sang *The Recessional* and just before the part about god's awful hand, which Tom thought was funny anyway, it got onto her neck. No one dobbed, but Miss Kennedy was watching them from the stage and she said they should be ashamed of themselves. If it wasn't Anzac Day tomorrow they'd have all been kept in.

'That's real nice,' says Gran now, folding up the red cape. 'Will you be going in for the march, then?' Gran won't go because of her feet. Pa was too old to fight even when the first war was on, and someone had to keep the cows milked, but he hasn't missed a march day since '46. And all the other Lovetts will be in it and the sisters' husbands and cousins and even some of the kids walk with their dads for part of the way.

'Would we be able to get a lift with Lionel or Ernie?' says Cathy, 'we're all right to get home.' Gran says just to call and see the boys at the bails on the way home because they'll be setting off pretty early in the morning. 'That's good,' says Cathy. 'Tom wants to see the Eyes Left part, so we'll have plenty of time to go over to the Memorial and get a good spot.' He's glad she didn't say Dad's coming down later with Mum and Nicholas so we can go for a swim. His dad never marches.

He'd rather get a lift with the Robinsons, but they'll be going to the Dawn Service for the Presbyterian address. So Mrs. Robinson and the Ladies Auxiliary can serve tea and biscuits at the RSL before the beer starts. She says it's a holy day and she doesn't like the men drinking and gambling. Just another excuse for the old boys to grog on his father says.

Dad doesn't drink beers much either. He's always too busy. He never seems to do the same things as the other dads in McClaren's Ridge. They wouldn't collect stamps or spend ages writing dates and headings on the pages of the albums in fancy writing and special ink. Or think Beethoven and ABC on the wireless is better than television. And he hardly even goes on the tractor any more now that he has to work at Carmichael's farm supplies and Harry shares the farm.

Well as long as it's not so squashed that he has to sit on Pa's knee in the car. Old Pa Lovett is a bit loud and cranky, but Mum says that's because he's nearly deaf. He doesn't call them the littlies. He knows all their names but he doesn't remember which one goes with which, so it doesn't matter how many of them he sees somewhere, he just waves and says 'HelloSusan-helloCathy-helloTom-andNickyWillams'. And Susan's not even here most of the time now. It's worse if he's by himself when Old Pa comes along, because then Pa grabs his hair or punches his shoulder and shouts out

107

'Whaddya know little tyke' and he always feels as though he doesn't know anything. Or 'look out for those joe blakes!' when he's wearing bare feet and he has to walk home.

Gran's lounge room is always pretty dim because of the curtains, so the faces on the wall seem to be looking out of the shadows. And the birds are a bit scary in the dark. There are two glass jars upside down on the china cabinet, with some leaves and branches inside them made to look like a garden or a toy forest. In one there are some tiny, bright birds like red and blue wrens and a big dry looking magpie with shiny eyes. He tries not to see the other one. There's an eagle hawk in there, with some dead prey animals underneath. Mice and things.

All the chairs have white covers with lace over the backs. On the cabinet too so the glass doesn't scratch. There are two armchairs and a couch, with sort of dressing gown cord along the corners and edges. The one he used to pretend was Father Bear's armchair is close to the bird jars, but that's the best spot. The big photos are leaning forward off the wall straight across the lounge room, so when the Vegemite kids or the ladies washing Persil whites come on the television, he can watch the soldiers.

He dreams that he's out there. Battling freezing nights in the African Desert and enduring the searing heat of the sun, sharing smokes and Red Cross parcels with Ernie and his mates. He marches through the streets of Greece to the cheers of local villagers, and he creeps through the sweaty green jungles of New Guinea and Borneo, clearing tracks with his machete, evading snipers. Sometimes his Division has to defend from trenches that they've dug with their bayonets and helmets or scraped out with the lids off bully beef tins ...

On the walls at home they've only got scenery – some paintings of Ayers Rock and the Outback, French trees with wavy sky, and some Japanese mountains.

Last year he couldn't even watch the march. They all went over to the School of Arts in Hartley – except for Nicholas, he was too little – because Cathy's mad about ballet. It was nearly the middle of the night when they came home. He wasn't going to stay home with his baby brother and April Robinson, so he had to go. Stupid *Swan Lake* and the Russian Boring Ballet. On Anzac Day. He remembers Dad saying Old Pa would love that, but he wouldn't.

It's Old Pa's chair, the Father Bear one, but that's all right. When he's walking over with Cathy, he always looks over to the shed and if Pa's not there helping with the milking, he sits somewhere else. Just in case Pa comes back early. It's brown velvet with stripes and swirls that feel smooth when you rub your fingers over it. And there's the silver ashtray on a stand with his pipe and Log Cabin tin. And the Kalinga Gazette. Pa reads Dagwood and Bluey and Curly and the funerals, but he gets angry at everything else in the newspaper. 'Place's going to the dogs,' he says. 'We fought to keep this country safe – now it's commies, common markets – hard enough to earn an honest quid, and now our butter's not good enough for the Queen.' And the Opera House. 'Stone the crows,' he says, 'five million now! Five million pounds of taxpayers' money on a ruddy opera house.'

Gran says 'don't take any notice of Pa. His bark's worse than his bite. Mr. Menzies won't let us down. He'll do the right thing by us.'

They're Gran's boys in the big pictures. She's got photos everywhere of cousins in weddings dresses and babies and people in frilly old clothes and braces, but only the soldiers are on the wall. Taken at the studio, she said. Young men, behind heavy glass, in dark polished frames with scrolly carving, hanging up with wire on special hooks like claws. Dressed in their uniforms with smooth faces and fresh haircuts, standing to attention and looking straight ahead, just before they went to The War. The soldiers that were Ernie and Lionel have big long frames with curly corners, and the other picture is oval shaped with vines and leaves carved into it. Cathy told him who they were.

You wouldn't think the first one was Ernie, because there's no roll-your-own out the side of his mouth and he looks very serious, but Gran said it was, and lovely he looked, in his khaki jacket and slouch hat. The soldier in the middle is wearing shiny, laced up boots and trying not to smile. That was a brother called Vince, who lives in Brisbane now and has to wear his trousers with one leg pinned up. The last one looks like young Dennis dressed up as an air force pilot, but that's because Dennis is Lionel's son and Lionel had more hair then and black.

He'd asked Gran about the soldiers and she showed him a velvet case she keeps in the cabinet drawer, with some buttons off their uniforms and rising sun badges and special medals they brought back from Africa and the Pacific. They've got Vol. Ten of Arthur Mee at home now so he could look up World War Two. There was a special chapter at the end called The Darkest Years of Our Century, but there wasn't much about Australia. Gran told him about Lionel defending the coast at Darwin and in the Coral Sea Battle, and Ernie in Africa and Greece. And how Vince got captured in Malaya and got gangrene.

Ernie told him a beaut story once about making rollies out of grass and vine leaves in Greece when they ran out of proper smokes. He tried that one time after the grapevine on the front verandah got going, but he nearly burnt his hair off at the front.

They can go with Ernie tomorrow morning. There'll be plenty of room in the truck because Old Pa's going in with Lionel and his family.

'Get a move on,' says Cathy, 'we'll cop it if we're late again.'

By the time they get back to their house, the sun will have gone – red sky at night – it should be a fine day for the march.

When his class got back to school today after the Anzac Assembly, Miss Kennedy talked about Gallipoli and the War the boys went to. Clifford James said his dad did the Kokoda Trail and he'd brought in a Japanese sword his father captured. Someone else said his father flew Catalina flying boats at Milne Bay when Australia beat the Japs. Steven's dad was a rat in Tobruk. Then Paul Morris started telling a story about when his uncle was a prisoner of war and him and his friends got vegetables off the Chinese by selling them petrol he stole out of a Jap officer's car, and Miss Kennedy said that's enough now and read some more war poems.

'Cathy?' He's been watching for snipers in the cutty grass, slicing at the air with the mark of Zorro to keep them at bay, and now he has to run to catch up, 'Was Dad ever in the War?'

'Of course he was. They all were.'

'He never talks about it.'

'I wouldn't either,' she says, 'it must've been horrible.'

'Can I swing the milk?' Ernie once showed them how to swing the bucket round and round when it was full of milk.

'No, you'll only spill it.'

It's turned out warm and sunny. Ernie's spread a blanket on the seat, and instead of tobacco and dust, the truck smells like mothballs, shoe polish and Californian Poppy. His feet are complaining already he says, and his suit's shrunk since last Anzac Day. 'Your Mum and Dad coming down later?' he asks Cathy, and she tells him Dad's just getting the crates finished so Harry can have some time off.

'Works too hard, Rob does,' he says. He lets them out near the Fire Station.

Everyone's lining up there in their groups – all the men in their suits and medals, the Boy Scouts and Girl Guides, the cadets, the High School band, and the Highlanders in their kilts. There's the

Red Cross girls, and Cheryl Lovett in Cathy's cape, and Mr. Robinson in his Anzac Day suit and medals from the first war. Cathy says he always likes to stay after morning tea on marching day.

'He might get a lift home with the Lovetts.'

'Over Old Pa's dead body,' Cathy says.

Someone is practicing the bagpipes and people are already lined up all along Oxley Street. As they hurry along to the Memorial the drum rolls start and he feels his shoulders go straight and his feet moving in time ...

Rob Williams is in the shed. With Easter so late this year, Hal Carmichael said 'Take the Tuesday off as well – start back after Anzac Day', so he's been able to give Harry a hand and they finished planting the beans in the first couple of days. And it's perfect weather. He's looking forward to washing off the week's work in the surf. Just knocking up a few banana cases now. There's only the one pallet of timber left now. After that it'll be all cardboard cartons.

He stacks another crate on the pile in the corner – they'll only need papering and lids for the next consignment – lines up the side boards with the last of the end pieces and hammers a nail into the soft, fresh wood ... *at the going down of the sun* ... he looks over to the little Ferris radio on the tool shelf ... *and in the morning* ... turns the crate on its end and hammers the other side, aware, suddenly of what is being broadcast ... *we will remember them* ... and the clear notes of the Last Post echo through the quiet stillness of the shed. His hands rest on the partly assembled case and images he'd rather leave in the past crowd Rob's mind – their father, reading the letters from Doug, Rob's youngest brother ...

" ... *Have finished my six weeks training on the Hurricanes and am now with a squadron ... we are a very cosmopolitan crowd. Two of the chaps have DFCs and you don't get those for nothing. I long for the day when I hope the King will be able to pin one on me. Ron and myself were rather unlucky a few days ago when we were not out with the squadron and they shot down a Hun. We were terribly envious but I suppose our chance will come ... Rob certainly got a quick call-up didn't he? And he did very well coming second out of eighty odd chaps on his course at Laverton. You must be very proud to have all four of us in it ...*

Since I last wrote we have been moved to another part of the country where we are having a very quiet time. However we hope to be back where there is plenty of action soon. The weather is beautiful at present and while I write this the sun is streaming down on me from a cloudless sky... one wouldn't think there was a war on. Our squadron is just like a "big lot of kids", always wrestling round in a scrimmage on the floor etc. You could not find a more happy- go-lucky mob ...

Dad, you finished your last letter by saying for me to look after myself. Please believe I am quite confident in looking after myself in the air ..."

... the letters their father received months after the squadron leader had written with the news that Sgt Pilot Douglas Williams, " *my number two, and one of our best pilots"*, had been shot down while making a low-level attack on a flack ship in the English Channel ... *"he will be sorely missed ...*

... and here's Rob, who wasn't his father's favourite son, and who didn't get shot down, eighteen years later. Time fades: it's '44 again, and he's flying the Anson back to base after another recovery operation, with his cargo of other families' sons and brothers and husbands, trying not to imagine all those stolen futures, but thinking, at least they'll be going home for burial ...

Tom stands to attention at the memorial. He waves his paper flag when the soldiers turn and salute. And when they bow their heads and hear the bugle and 'age shall not weary them', he sees the men on the wall, brave and proud with their smiling eyes and pressed uniforms, going off to war and never growing old.

Kalinga, School Holidays 1963

CATHY

'SO, WHAT'S IT like?' I said. Hoping she'd go on about how awful the new school was and how she'd be coming back to Kalinga High after all.

Christine was home for the September holidays and I was staying at Garvey's for the weekend.

'Wonderful,' she said. 'We still have English and Maths and everything, you know, for matriculation, but every day we have a Modern Etiquette period.'

'Modern etiquette?' I said, thinking, this will be funny. But she was pretty serious.

'You know, how to comport yourself in social situations. Setting up a home, entertaining, how to make a happy and successful marriage.' She actually said *comport*. I had to look it up when I got home.

'Needlework too, but it's so much better,' she said, 'not just fringed placemats and shortie pyjamas. We draft patterns and learn about style, accessorizing outfits for different occasions.'

They had religious instruction nearly every day too, but most of it was good. She'd had to do a bit more thinking about the sorts of things we were meant to prepare for at confirmation, she said, but it all makes us a better person. Listening to her reminded me a bit of Denise Hunt when she was in full flight on *The Swing*, at elocution. I wished I hadn't told her about not being baptised. I haven't ever told her about Melvin. She always thought Michael Thompson was a bit hopeless, so she'd think Melvin was really weird.

114

'We'll go over to the beach later,' she said, 'it's too windy now. You have to come and see my bedroom. Dad had it redecorated for my birthday surprise.'

It was lovely. It looked just like the *Make your Teenager's Bedroom a Place to Dream In* page from Garvey's Spring Catalogue. She even had Venetian blinds and her own dressing table with a three-piece mirror. Then we went through the built-in wardrobe and all the new outfits she'd been putting together. When Mrs. Garvey goes up to Brisbane, she and Christine have shopping trips to McWhirters and MacDonnell and East. She had a new swimming costume too, one of the ones with a knife-pleated overblouse and built in cups. Watermelon pink. I thought about my Speedos and hoped it would stay cloudy.

It's funny when you stay at other people's places. Because it's not home, you can't just go into your room and read if you feel like it, or even tidy up, maybe grab a piece of fruit and sit in the mango tree and think about things. So you look forward to the meals. The way you do when you're on holiday and there's not a lot else to do or think about except rubbing raw tomato on your sunburn before you go to bed, or whether someone will say let's go to the pictures, or is it too soon after lunch to go swimming again. You see someone putting an interesting looking brown paper bag in the cupboard when they come back from getting the newspaper and you think, terrific, maybe apple cake, or iced buns for afternoon tea.

And it's always exciting to see what other people's mothers cook. Well, usually.

Lunch was pretty disappointing. I'd been hoping it would be something like grilled cheese and tomato on toast, fish and chips, or even hamburgers, because the Garveys lived right near the beach. They had a paved entertaining area and their own brick barbeque in the back yard just like the ones at the camping ground, with a new outdoor setting from Garvey's Furniture Emporium and everything, and Mrs. Garvey had to say how fortunate they were – so handy to the beach, but never bothered by mosquitoes.

When lunch came, it was thick, lumpy pink slices of Camp Pie, some tomatoes, lettuce and cucumber. Then Mr. Garvey whipped the brown paper bag out of the cupboard and said 'Mustn't forget this!' He put a sliced tank loaf on the bench. 'Don't be shy, missy,' he said, 'tuck in.'

We did go over to the beach after lunch. We put swimmers on, but under our Bermudas and blouses because it was still a bit cool. 'Why don't you get a training bra,' Christine said when we were getting changed. 'You might grow faster.' Better for your posture too, she said.

She picked a nice private spot in the dunes out of the wind, where we could sunbake. Not long after, a couple of really cute boys from the Surf Club came down to say hi. They knew Christine because they went to the boys' school next door to hers in Brisbane. They were pretty nice, but they all knew a lot of people I didn't know, and I felt like they'd have been talking about different stuff if I wasn't there.

I was nearly embarrassed enough to go for a swim, but I'd rather have died than expose my speedos and white legs to the world. Not to mention theoops-I'm-sorry-I-forgot-to-grow lumps that are meant to be a Bust. Mum says I should be grateful I don't have to worry about All That yet. She doesn't have to be the stick insect in the showers after P.E. Anyway, there weren't any flags and you get bluebottles with an easterly.

So the next thing to look forward to was dinner.

Once, when I was flicking through Mum's *Commonsense Cookery Book*, I came across the word "fricassee". I remembered what an ugly word I thought it was, watching what must be boiled onions and something fricasseed on the plates Christine's mother was passing round. The sort of plates you always break when you're at someone else's house. With a country scene in the middle, that you could discover gradually as you ate.

Dinner in the Garvey household turned out to be very polite, so no hints emerged in general conversation … *Yummy, I love___ stew!* Or *Oh, Mum, not ___ again!* Chicken I guessed, but everyone else must have got all the meat. Most of the lumps in my white sauce seemed to be skin – or rubbery squares of gristle. The only way I could eventually swallow them was by pretending they were onions too.

By the time I had exposed my dancing shepherdesses, everyone else had finished, and what I hoped didn't look like a lot of food was carefully arranged around the edge of my plate. Some of it was meant to look like sheep.

'That was really nice, Mrs. Garvey,' I said. 'I just never eat much.'

So the serving of red jelly I got was so small that for a long time I could still only taste and smell quivery white things.

'Tripe!' Mum said, when I tried to describe what we'd had. 'Heavens above.'

Occasionally, at our house, crumbed brains appear, pretending to be small meatballs. Tom and Nicky still think they're all right. But since Mum hates tripe too, I'd never seen it on a dinner plate. One of the dreaded internal organs – tongues, and kidneys and all those other gleaming, sometimes even bristly collections of innards that I'd studied in the butcher's display case, but could never imagine anyone eating.

Well, I know what tripe is now, and what it looks like fricasseed. But I can almost still say I have never eaten it. I tried.

'I saw Christine again,' I said to Diane, when we got back after the holidays. 'I stayed at Garveys' for the weekend. It was really nice.'

'Has she got stuck up?' Diane asked.

I thought about lying in the dark in Christine's apricot bedroom with the ivory trim. Still feeling slimy, cold lumps at the back of my throat, and not being game to ask her what on earth we'd had for tea.

'Of course not,' I said.

Part Five

Moments in childhood

"There is always one moment in childhood when
The door opens and lets the future in."
Graham Greene; 'The Power and the Glory'

McClaren's Ridge, June 1960

CATHY

SO, NOW I'M in High School. And I did get picked for the debating team. Thanks a lot Sister Marie Agnes. Denise did too, but everyone knew she would. Christine's gone to Brisbane. To an all girls' school where they do more on deportment and social graces. Her mum wants her to try out for June Dally Watkins.

I go on the bus most days now, because it's nice for Tom to have someone to go with.

I got my elocution Certificate.

I told Mum about the exam after I got home that day, and how I was worried that I wouldn't remember it all but I did, and how Sister Marie Agnes said good girl after I'd finished so I should pass. I said it's probably best if I come home on the bus now that Elocution's finished and it's getting dark early. Kenny talked a lot I said and it was a bit hard to get away – *Do you like keeping secrets* he said – so if she wins any more prizes I said, maybe Dad wouldn't mind going to collect them.

I told Christine about Johnny Buckley and the inkwells, but I said by the time we finished Elocution it was too late and I never got to meet Kenny Fisher after all.

There are some things you just can't tell anyone.

There are a few things I'd like to tell Melvin, but I don't think Mum and Dad would like it. Of all the cousins that might have come for a holiday, it had to be Melvin.

'It's only small, isn't it,' he said when we got to the Bird Sanctuary.

120

But he ran on ahead with his ten-shilling note and pushed through the turnstiles before Tom or I could get close enough to trip him.

Tom called out after him, 'You forgot your snake stick, Melvin.'

'Lorikeets can be pretty dangerous when provoked,' I said.

And Dad said, 'That's enough, you two.'

Before Dad could show them round the farm yesterday, Melvin and Uncle Harold spent ages whittling Sally Wattle branches into stout walking prods with Melvin's new all-purpose pocket knife. To attack brown snakes when they leapt out from the long grass.

He brought his junior binoculars today. 'Binoculars!' I said, 'this is The Bird Century, Melvin. You might get a bird's eye view of a bird's eye.'

'Tom used to think it was called The Century,' I added, before Melvin could explain the actual meaning of the word "sanctuary" for me, 'because there were hundreds of birds.'

'We'll find him,' says Dad. 'Couldn't miss that shirt.' Red and green palm trees.

Dad likes Melvin though, because Melvin's always saying things like 'Excuse me, Uncle Rob, what's the acreage here?' and 'Any blight from the frosts?' He even insisted on paying his own way into the Sanctuary. 'That's what my holiday money's for, Uncle Rob, and I know things are difficult in the banana industry at the moment.'

'Well excuse me, Melvin,' I thought, 'while I go and vomit.'

We've been to The Sanctuary a million times, but as usual, Dad wants to do educational things. Even when people are supposed to be on holiday. So far we haven't done anything that Melvin hasn't already seen or done better in Sydney. Taronga Park's got a lot more animals than just a few porpoises, Genevieve was about the only interesting car at Gilltrap's Auto Museum, and he got gastric when we went to The Golden Pagoda.

But he agreed with Dad that the Sanctuary would be a good idea. And of course he already knew that lorikeets have special brushes on their tongues for collecting nectar.

Mum's probably sorry she said she'd stay behind with Nicky at the El Dorado. I've never seen inside a motel before and we thought we might swim in the kidney-shaped pool, but you could see it was going to be a quiet sort of afternoon. Aunty Jean's got a 'frightful head coming on', and Uncle Harold's 'already *puce*, he'll be peeling by tomorrow!' Probably because he spent all morning trying to beat Melvin at putt-putt.

'Don't take your hat off, Melvin,' Aunty Jean said to him, patting a folded handkerchief into his walk shorts, 'and look out for mosquitoes.'

Mum said, 'We don't get mozzies at this time of year.' But something's bitten him. Above the long socks and below the tropical shirtsleeves, his legs and arms are all spotted with these blodgy looking patches of Calamine lotion. I'll die if we see anyone from school.

'Plenty of time, folks,' the ranger said, trying to pass tin plates to everyone, 'no pushing,' and to Melvin, who was holding up the line, 'There'll be birds, sonny, mark my words. They like red, too,' he grinned, eyeing Melvin's shirt.

We got a good spot on the fence, near the birds' Ferris wheel, and more rangers came round with buckets of syrupy gruel for the feed dishes. 'Where are all the birds?' he said. 'When mother and dad took me to Myall Lakes …'

'Shut up, Melvin,' I told him, 'they'll be here.'

'Yeah,' said Tom, 'shut up Melvin.'

'There are no birds, Uncle Rob.'

Beside us, a little boy who'd been studying Melvin's palm trees, suddenly crumpled and set up a wailing chant: 'No birds, Mummy. No birds!'

In my mind's eye, Melvin was blotted out of existence by The Blob from Outer Space, crushed by a falling tea tree, sucked into the air by a freak tornado – and just as I was dreaming it, the whirlwind got louder and closer – the sound of a million tin whistles split the afternoon, and the sky was beating with screeches and flashes of colour. The trees were covered in rippling blankets of emerald, vermilion and electric blue. Then all at once, as if somewhere a referee blew his whistle, the blanket lifted and the lorikeets rose in a shrieking clatter, took aim and dived down onto the plates and arms all round the edge of the grass oval.

Spangly beads of sweet water laced the air. Beating wings stirred up gusts of tea tree blossom, coconut oil and nectar, and over all of us, there was a roar of excitement and screams and laughter mixed with the scratch and chatter of the feeding birds.

I suddenly realized I'd never seen Melvin laugh before.

'Up till now,' he said, 'it's always been my experience that nothing's as good as you think it's going to be.'

He'd stripped off his socks and sandals and was wriggling his pink and white ribbed toes on the car floor, scuffing his feet in the farm dust and the sand and Tom's shell collection from last Christmas. His arms were speckled with cereal and dried nectar bread.

'We'd better get you cleaned up, tiger,' Dad said.

'Can we go to the beach, Uncle Rob? Can I wash it off in the surf? I don't care about stingers and undertows.'

And under his breath, 'I hope I *get* sun burnt.'

When we finally got him back to the El Dorado, Aunty Jean lowered her dark glasses and sank back on the banana lounge. 'Oh, Melvin,' she said.

Fred Lang was there, at the Sanctuary, taking photos. Melvin was in one, so we went to the studio to pick it up before they went to the airport. It was all right, he stands out, but it was taken before the birds came.

We've got a photo too. Dad took it later, with our Box Brownie. Tom and I have got our arms around Melvin – he's got lorikeets on his shoulders and all over the metal dish he's holding up, bread and honey in his hair and a big grin on his face. I said we'd give him a copy next time he comes up. We're going to be pen pals.

McClaren's Ridge, February 1958

TOM

THERE WERE LOTS of jobs for him on the farm. Mum let him watch when she was working in the shed. When she put the tomatoes into all their special sizes and colours on the big table which was grading, and packed the crates and then put the letters on with stencils and black ink. And it was his own special job to shoo the stupid cows away when they got too close to the shed. He could help the pickers too, going along the furrows in between the beans, but being careful not to walk on the plants. Sometimes Dulcie or Maureen gave him some beans to put in the bags or he could eat little ones but not too many or you'll spoil your tea.

The best thing was helping Dad in the cultivation and learning all the names for everything. It was a Ferguson tractor. Some of the things you could only watch, like loading the heavy fertilizer bags onto the trailer and putting the Disk Harrows on, but sometimes Dad let him ride carefully on the back of the tractor and he could watch the big tyres pressing fish-bone lines into the red soil and see the plough cutting the long straight furrows for the new crops.

One time Adamson's bulldozer came to clear some land for a new paddock. It was a Caterpillar and it had Treads instead of tyres. They didn't have any Front-End-Loaders or Semi-Trailers or Backhoes or Tip-Trucks at the farm, but he saw them working at the quarry and other places, and he already had some of these at home because Matchbox Toys were the special presents he always got for birthdays and Christmas. Or Tonka toys for very special. He didn't have a Post-Hole Digger, but he knew what it was.

125

It was to do with the Lectricity. Dad had shown him all the poles along Oxley Street when they went into town and Mum said now she'd be able to switch on the washing machine they'd brought all the way up from Melbourne. Instead of using it to ripen bananas in and thank god with all the nappies.

Lots of new things were happening. There was a new baby, and Tom wasn't trying to hurt him, but whenever he tried to play with him everyone said be careful and don't hurt him because he's only little.

The Post-Hole Digger is here to make holes for our electricity poles, Dad told him. Mum said Keep right away from the workmen and the machinery, it's too dangerous, but Dad said He'll be all right, just be very careful, Tom. And he told the men to watch out for him.

Each morning he waited for the roar of the engines and watched the Digger working. When the men had their smoko he sat under the trees in the shade with them. Don't half ask a lot of questions for a little tyke, they said but they told him things about why you had to dig such deep holes for the Lectricity poles. So he watched as more holes were dug and special flat lids like big wooden wheels were put over the ones that were finished but still waiting to be filled in with poles. Dad invented those. He said if you cut the tops and bottoms off the Lectricwire rolls they'd be just the right size and they were.

Soon he could follow the trail of the lids, right from the mailbox at the bottom of the gravel road up Lovett's hill, down to the lantana gully then up the hill to home. He could see where all the lines and wires would go, along the tops of the poles. They would be like a line of soldiers marching up to the house.

The diggers had gone and the poles would be coming soon. The dangerous machinery had gone, so he decided he would be a

Newalectricline and join up each hole. All the way from the mail-box to the house. It was like playing Fly. Trying to see if you could take really long jumps and get there in two steps instead of three. Except with the poles, it was a giant game. More like twenty two steps instead of twenty three. And he could nearly count to a hundred already, even though he was only four, so it was easy.

He galloped past Lovett's in case Pop came out and said whaddya know liddlefella then he cantered up the hill after the gully because he wanted to beat the girls home and tell them all about being the electricity wires. Before they got busy with the baby and their other jobs.

There was only the last hole to go. Now he was on a fiery steed, with the speed of light. He fired a warning shot with his pistols, shouted Hi-Ho Silver, and he and his horse leapt onto the lid.

He saw the gap as he was jumping.

The cover flipped sharply, like a giant coin. The ground fell away and his world went black.

MARGARET

SHE CAME IN from the shed about half past four. She hated having to take Nicholas with her, but if she couldn't help with the packing, they'd never get this lot of beans in and loaded on time.

Cathy and Susan fussed over the baby while she splashed the dust and sweat off her face and hands at the sink and got ready for his five o'clock feed. Thankfully the girls had already cut kindling for the stove and started the vegetables.

Electricity – God, she was counting the days till they could flick a switch and kiss goodbye to all the kero lamps, wicks and mantles. Probably never get the smoke stains of the walls though. Still, no more wrestling blocks of ice, fishing great tangled lumps of steaming sodden laundry out of the copper.

'Where's Tom, Mum?' asked Cathy.

'With Dad. Over in the back paddock. They should be back soon. Susan, can you go over now and pick up the milk? And Cathy, don't annoy Nicky when he's feeding. If you have your bath now, you can help Tom when he comes in.'

Shortly after, she heard Rob knocking the mud of his boots on the back step. 'Rob, can you tell Tom to go and have his bath now? Cathy should be just about finished.'

'Where is he?'

She went to the back door. 'What do you mean? I thought he was with you.'

'No. I haven't seen him all afternoon love – he was at the paddock this morning but then I thought he came back here.'

'He's usually in by now. It'll be dark soon.' She hefted the drowsy baby onto her hip, went out to the front verandah and called, 'To – om … tea time!'

'I'd better go and get him,' said Rob. 'He's probably gone to meet me and I missed him on the way back. Get the girls to go and check Robinsons and Lovetts.'

'Susan's gone to Lovett's to get the milk. He might come back with her.'

Rob laced his boots. 'I'll go anyway, just in case. Cathy, can you run up to Robinson's and see if he's there?'

Margaret went back out to the verandah.

She knew that Gran or Mrs. Robinson would have sent him home before this. The shadows were lengthening, and it was already quite dark down in the gully. These days of late summer were long, but when night fell, it was sudden. She called him again, but could only hear the echo of her own voice and the growing hum of cicadas in the warm, windy dusk.

She held the baby tightly to her breast and rubbed her face over his dark downy hair. 'Where is he, Nicky? Where's my other baby?' She laid him in the bassinet and secured the little mosquito net.

Back in the darkening kitchen, she put the saucepan of beans to the side of the stove and lit the lamps, using the last match to light a cigarette, which she hoped would help stop her hands shaking. Chilled, despite the heat, she pulled on her old shed cardigan and hugged her arms across her stomach, waiting.

Rob came back alone. Tom wasn't with Cathy or Susan either, but the neighbours had come to help find him and search parties were formed. The first time someone suggested checking the postholes, everyone said, 'No, that's not likely – that timber's really heavy …'

As it was, there were only the ones closest to their house that Rob'd had to seal till the power company came back. First place he'd checked, he said.

No one wanted to think that he might have crossed the big road down at the mail box. Not yet. If searching had to be done in the bush on the other side, ropes and pulleys would be needed. And it was not the sort of searching that could be done at night.

So they went on, all over Robinson's, Lovett's and their own paddocks, down to the creek and back ...

TOM

HE TRIED TO climb up, but everything was cold and slippery and he couldn't see where to climb to.

He had called so long his voice was sore. He heard his Dad, but it couldn't have been, because when he said I'm down here get me out the voice outside got further away.

He didn't know if it was dark everywhere and already teatime. Maybe the new baby needed feeding.

No one came.

He had stopped trying to climb out. If he stayed still he might hear someone.

And if there were spiders and snakes maybe they would keep still too …

He hadn't moved at all for a long time but he still couldn't hear anyone.

He thought he heard his mother call him for tea but when he called out again no one was there …

And his voice hurt.

MARGARET

IT WAS EIGHT o'clock before they found him.

It was dark, but the wind had dropped. Distraught, she'd begged the men to check the post holes again. 'I know it seems impossible, but please – at least we'll know', and as soon as Rob and Harry knelt to heft the cover off a hole barely a hundred yards from the back of the house, calling to Tom as they did so, Rob yelled 'Christ, I think he is down there! He's here, love – quick ...'

'Oh God,' she cried, 'I knew it – is he ...'

Even when they dragged the cover away, Tom was barely visible, six feet below, huddled and whimpering at the bottom of that smooth narrow chimney in the ground. The sun had gone out of his face ... the bloody farm ... this bloody house – it wasn't even safe enough to have electricity connected, according to the power company. That's why those holes weren't finished ... and now this ...

He was clenched tight, quivering and streaked with cold dark clay.

'I called out,' he sobbed, 'but everyone had gone. I didn't mean to fall down the hole.'

'It's all right now little man, we've got you,' said Rob.

She knelt beside the posthole and wrapped him close in her cardigan and a blanket someone had passed down. 'Don't cry sweetie, you're all right now.'

'I *wanted* you Mum.'

Everyone was talking at once, 'No bones broken – not a scratch on him – it's amazing.'

'Thank heavens he landed feet first!'

'Jeez, why didn't any of us hear him before this though?'

'Maybe he was out to it for a while. Hole's so deep – sealed up like that – and the wind ...'

'It had to be the wind ... I thought I heard him, it was the first place I looked – but I could have sworn it was coming from the scrub ...'

'Blimey, how long do you reckon he was down there?'

Rob was thanking all the neighbours. They wouldn't stay for cups of tea – must get home for dinner, and Tom wants a good hot bath and bed. 'He's a tough little bloke,' he said, 'aren't you mate? He'll be right.'

Tom was clinging to her, face buried in her neck, his small swaddled figure still shuddering with cold and sobs. 'Nice hot bath for you, Sweetie chops, then toast soldiers, story and beddie byes. No more shivers.' She rose and handed him up to Rob.

He looked over Rob's shoulder as he carried him in.

'Nobody came,' he said.

TOM

THEY SAID IT was eight o'clock when they found him. Big hand on the twelve and the little one on the eight. Like after breakfast, only the other eight o'clock, after bedtime. When it's dark. But he knew when he saw the stars that there are places even darker than nighttime.

Lots of people had been looking, but it was a long time before they picked the right place. Harry and Dad pulled him out and everyone said what a brave boy he was.

After his tea he had *The Teddy Bear's Picnic* which was his favourite song, and that night's chapter of *Winnie-the-Pooh* and Mum rubbed Vicks on his chest just in case. She tucked him in, but he woke up later because he was having a nightmare about cold dark places where he couldn't move. Where Mummies and Daddies didn't come in time to take you home to bed.

A lot more things have happened since the electricity came.

Susan has gone to the city to study. Mum and Cathy have to watch the baby even more now because he's started walking and there still isn't much Tom can do to help. And his Dad will be going to go away from the farm each day to work. To get enough money to feed them all he says. Until their ship comes in. But although Tom watches the horizon each day, the sea seems to be too far away from their house for a ship to ever get there.

It's like living in a different place and being someone else. He doesn't care about the electricity. He doesn't even like big trucks and heavy machinery much anymore. School is good, but his favourite thing is reading the Arthur Mees, because he can find out all sorts of things and he doesn't have to worry about asking people when they're too busy.

Sometimes Mum and Dad have to take him back to bed in the night because he wakes up and he's out on the verandah, or walking somewhere that he doesn't know. And sometimes he's a bit scared to go back to sleep in case the dream comes back.

And he knows that most of the time, it's no use calling out, because nobody will be able to hear him.

Kalinga, July 1959

CATHY

I WAIT TILL Mr. Jackson turns to write more action word exercises on the board, and pass my note across the aisle to Christine. Just to let her know that I still have my secret appointment for this afternoon after Elocution.

I ride my bike most days now instead of going on the bus, so I can stay after school for tunnel ball practice or go round to Christine Garvey's place for a while. But I take elocution on Fridays. She sends the note back and says make sure I remember everything so I can tell her next week.

Christine's been my best friend since fourth class when she started new at our school, and we tell each other everything. She's got really tan skin without even having to sun bake much, and her Aunty manages the Cut'n'Curl so Christine and her cousin Kay always have the latest Richard Hudnut styling solutions. "Lovelier, more natural looking curls". For the first few weeks though, or whenever they go swimming, they look more like wet Poodles. So I don't want a perm, but one of the first things I do want when I grow up is to get pierced ears for sleepers, even though I know I'll probably faint. Christine says it didn't hurt at all.

I told her how I really want to be a ballet dancer and that another thing I'm going to do when I'm old enough is change my name to Carole or something ending in "ette" – like *Odette* on the radio serial. "The true story of a very brave woman". Christine even knows about the time I spent all my lunch money on love lollies and then ate them all myself under the desk because I wasn't game to send them to Michael Thompson. She told me how when Kay was supposed to take her to see *King Creole* one Saturday night, Kay put lipstick and eye shadow on and went next door to the Dance Palais after the serial. Then Christine got a milkshake at interval and Alan Clark asked her to sit up the back with him and he was already in high school. He had cigarettes too, and she said she had a puff but it was awful.

The other day she said 'Mum says I'm going to another school after Primary. She reckons there's too much bad influence here.'

'What am I going to do when you go?' I said, 'You're my best friend.' I mean, we get round with Diane and Pam as well, but it'll be awful without Christine.

'She wants me to learn etiquette and everything. I think we have to go to church every day too. Or chapel or something. I haven't been since I got confirmed.'

'You know what,' I said, 'you know when I stopped going to confirmation classes?' And I told her about not being baptised. I made the story a bit more interesting. I said it was because Mum and Dad were moving around a lot from Sydney to Melbourne with his job and everything, but she didn't think it was weird at all.

Where I'm going after Elocution is not really a secret, but I haven't told anyone except Christine about that because they'd think I was just skiting.

All the other girls, well just about, the ones who live in town anyway, are in the Girl Guides. Some of them wear their uniforms with the belts and sashes and everything on Wednesdays because they meet after school at the Scout Hall. And Denise Hunt makes us play Guides at lunchtime.

Denise has got tickets on herself. She went down to Sydney to see Billy Graham. I said some of my relatives saw the Queen Mother in Canberra, but she wasn't that impressed. I suppose seeing Billy Graham makes you a more *confident, self-respecting, responsible com-*

munity member. Well soon she won't be the only person who knows someone famous.

Anyway, she's bagged a special part of the playground near the Sevenies wall and on Wednesdays, instead of Rounders, we all have to do Journey Challenges and be *wide awake and do our best*. Christine said Denise is trying to be the first one in their Brownie Pack to get her Link Badge to Guides, but a new girl from Pelican Point Primary got voted to be pack leader, so now Denise has to boss us around at school.

The Brownie uniform is nice, but I don't like camping much, and anyway, if I can't do the Pow Wow sign properly it's no good. Putting two fingers straight to the ground in the Pow Wow circle if you want to speak. I kept bending my middle finger because it's a lot longer than the next one, and Denise said 'Well that's not right. Look, everyone else can do it'. So I'd just be embarrassed at Guides. And they'll soon be going into navy uniforms, which aren't as nice as the brown ones.

There's only one other girl from our class that goes to Elocution, and it has to be Denise. Mum wanted me to go because I might have adenoids and because at Parents and Teachers Day, Mr. Stockbridge said I was a good student and I could be a good debater, but I'm a bit shy. It would help me talk up in class and be more confident he said, and that now before I go into high school would be a good time, especially if I ever wanted to go into teaching.

One last thing I want to do is be on the debating team and the other last thing is be a teacher, but Elocution's a chance to get out of chopping the wood on Fridays and I like learning poems. Before Susan went to college she used to teach me some of her really good high school ones when we were doing the dishes. *Ozymandias* and the *Inchcape Rock*. Or we'd pretend to be the ancient mariner – water, water, everywhere – clack the cutlery for the highwayman galloping, until Mum would say 'Cut it out in there, you two'.

Most of the ones we do at elocution are a bit babyish, but I still like going. We have to go round to St. Xavier's because Sister Marie Agnes teaches us. It's interesting seeing inside their school. It's not as different as I thought it might be. Mostly pictures of Jesus on the wall instead of the Queen, and lots of crosses, but their desks are just like ours, with inkwells and everything. Well, usually I like going. The only trouble is we've got Certificate exams today, so I've got butter-flies about that, as well as meeting a famous person off the wireless.

Which is what I'm doing after Elocution. I'm going to meet Kenny Fisher.

He's in Brisbane now, but old Mrs. Fisher still lives in the big house on Fig Tree Hill. She doesn't get about much. People say Kenny comes home every so often because she's not a well person and he's all she's got, but no one I know has ever seen him. All the kids listen to *Kenny's Korner* every afternoon. *Music for Moderns* is on later, at the same time Jack Davey is on the local radio station with the Vincent's Show, so not many people know that Mum's always winning the *Name That Tune* quiz.

It's hard not to tell Denise about Kenny saying to Mum that he'd be coming down for the weekend, so he'd bring the records she won and I'm going to pick them up from the Fishers' house. 'We live a bit out of town,' Mum told them, 'but Cathy rides her bike on Fridays and Fig Tree Hill is on her way home.' When I told Christine, I said I won't say anything to the other kids till afterwards. They might just think I'm making it up or showing off, I said.

Sister Marie Agnes is really nice and she loves poetry, but when she's talking it's a bit like watching a spitting horse. Some of the Catholic kids do elocution too, but they've usually finished when we get there, so it's just Denise and me and Sister Marie Agnes's teeth. We've been practicing *The Swing* for the exam. Robert Louis Steven-son must have been having a rest after *Kidnapped* and *Treasure Island*, but at least it's not very long. Lots of RISing and FALLing, so we can really enUNciate, and FEEL the uu-UPZZ and DO- ownzz – 'Pictyor yourthelf ON the sthwing' she says.

Denise is pretty good at this because she thinks she's some sort of actress and she takes everything so seriously. 'Sister,' she asks, 'should we say: "How do you like to go up in a SWING", or "How do YOU like to go up in a swing"?' And each time she's finished and standing there smiling at a place on the back wall with her feet together, Sister Mary Agnes really goes to town on the EXScellents.

Then I go, trying not to think of falling OFF the swing and teeth spraying everywhere, but I usually have to try twice and I get the giggles and don't really put enough oomph into it. 'Again dear,' she says, 'Light ath air – FEEL the sswing! – whoosssh!' – spit – and I start to even forget the lines. I think of all the other poems I know, and all the s's come leaping out. *Wessstminssster Bridge, Daffodilsss.* The main bits of *The Highwayman* would be fairly safe, but it's too many verses to get through without laughing.

Mum knows. She thinks it's pretty funny too, but it's all for my own good to speak from the chest. I mean DIAphragm. Most times when I practice *The Swing* at home with all the actions, enunciating "Oh, I DO think it the pleasantest thing Ever a child can do!" through my after school Weetbix and Vegemite, we all end up laughing, especially when I put on my class pet performance. But I know Mum wants me to do well in the Certificate. I do too I suppose. I don't think I'll ever be able to swim as fast as Ilsa Konrads and by the time they get ballet classes in Kalinga I'll be too old to get on the road to fame that way.

I think I'll be all right. I just hope it doesn't take too long, because some of the Xavier's kids are doing their exam today too, and I don't want to be late getting to Fishers' place. Christine said I should ask Kenny for an autograph, or maybe even get a signed picture, but I think I'd be too embarrassed to do that. 'What am I going to say to him,' I said, and she said 'I don't know, just talk about how we all like *Kenny's Korner*, and how does he remember all those jokes. Ask him what it's like to be a famous radio person and everything.'

So I've reached the bottom of Fig Tree Hill and I'm making up interesting questions. Maybe I could recite The Swing. See if there might be radio careers for people who don't like talking in public.

At least the exam's all over. It was good and bad. We had to take turns sitting out in the hall while the others were in the room with Sister Agnes and another examiner sister. That was good, because I couldn't see how excellent Denise's enunciation was, and because sitting there with all the names of excellent students from the past and pictures of Saints and Mary and Jesus looking down on you, it was hard not to feel serious. I mean He died specially for us and everything, so you could at least try. Bad too though, because the longer you sat there, the more nervous you got – well I did – trying to practice the right lines in my head. I kept getting blocked with "Our Father, Harold be thy name" and shepherds washing their socks by night. If I tried to concentrate on picturing myself on the swing, instead of describing a joyful arc "up in the air so blue", my brain started galloping urgently – riding, riding, riding; up to the old Inn Door.

I'll probably pass. I mean you'd have to be pretty dreadful not to. I did remember it all and I kept my chin up and didn't move my hands too much. Gosh, it's only the Preparatory.

Johnny Buckley was in one of the classrooms, writing "I must not plug the inkwells with blotting paper" all over the blackboard. He goes on our bus sometimes if his mum's not working at the fish shop and he once asked me if I was going to the Saturday Matinee. He said 'What are *you* doing here Williams?' and I said 'Nothing, *Buck*ley.'

Maybe Kenny can tell me how to think up smart answers.

141

I'm going to ask him if he can play *Señor Onion* more often. It's the best story and I only ever heard it once. About a Spanish onion who rolls along the road singing opera and Lady of Spain and things. He wants to fall in love, but whenever he meets ze ladees, zey start to cry.

By the time I've climbed all the steps to Mrs. Fisher's verandah I've got more nervous than I was for the exam. It's nearly dark too because of all the camphor laurels and Moreton Bay figs around the house. I don't think anyone's heard me knocking, but suddenly he's there.

He's much taller than he sounds on *Kenny's Korner* – big and squishy. He's wearing a baggy, grey sort of furry cardigan and I think about those underground animals that only come out at night, snuffling round for a meal of smaller furry animal. Because he's peering through the these glasses like the bottom of a jar that make his eyes look big and round and he has to lean forward as if he's sniffing the air to touch my arm with his big damp hand like a pink paw.

'Cathy,' he says, 'what a pretty name for a pretty girl. Do you like music too?'

I can't remember whether I like music or not. I can't remember any of the things we were going to talk about.

'Come on through,' he says, and takes me down the dark hallway that smells like cats and mothballs and into the living room and there's piles of old newspapers and 78's stacked up in the corners. On top of the radiogram there's one of those dolls with a knitted skirt that usually sit on bedspreads. I thought he'd have music on, but it's pretty quiet. He's wearing slippers too.

He doesn't look much like a famous person at all.

On the wireless he sounds like a small, happy young man with a deep voice. I know he's got some sort of problems because he's nearly albino. He left Kalinga to get treatment. It was good that he'd

142

done so well for himself people said – a hard life as a kiddy, but such a lovely person and so generous – do anything for his old mum and just adores children.

Actually, I thought old Mrs. Fisher might be there but she must already be in bed or something. When he says I can't go without a glass of milk and a bit of a chinwag he's got some really nice biscuits and he's sure my mum wouldn't mind if I stay for just a little while, he sounds as if he might be getting a cold and I don't really want to, but he might be lonely and it was so good of him to say I could pick up Mum's quiz prize at his place instead of mum or dad having to go to the Radio Station. So I say I'll have a biscuit but I'll have to go soon and I can't ruin my tea and when he says did my mum knit my jumper and can he look closer and it would be better if I sit nearer to him because he can't see me properly I'm not game to be rude to him and those soft hands are really strong so I think well all right I'll just sit on his knee and have one more biscuit …

By the time I get to Whipbird Creek I've worked out how to sit on my bike so it doesn't hurt because I'm getting tired having to pedal standing up all the way. If I can't feel it I can stop feeling ashamed about not being game to tell him to stop touching me like that and just plain embarrassed about him being so weird. If I stop thinking about it I can forget it.

When cars cross the bridge now they don't have to slow down and think about anything. You might as well still be on the road, because it's all so smooth it doesn't make any noise or feel bumpy under the wheels. They won't let kids go fishing or diving off there anymore.

Except for Ruby, and that awful time when it was just the poles, going over the river used to be like going over to a separate place.

McClaren's Ridge, Winter 1960

SUSAN

THE FIRST YEAR away, she came home every holiday. It would still stop her breath when she saw Danny, crouched in the curl of a wave, striding up the beach. They'd talk, sometimes go to the pictures; go for drives. He'd talk about surfing and she tried to make college and city life sound like something else you could be interested in.

He'd started working for his dad, but spent most of his time getting to be a champion on the board he finally owned. 'Be a while before I have to bring the bacon home to anyone,' he said.

'I'm gunna set up a surf shop, make boards. Gunna go travelling in the comps when I get me own car.' He'd be holding her hand, but he'd be staring at the ocean. 'There's nothing like it,' he'd say, 'When the swells start far out on the horizon. That's when the feeling starts. And you lie there and see the sets rolling in, closer and closer and then you know the next one is the one, and you get up on your knees and feel that wave pull you back, and up – and then the board gets its own momentum.'

When he talked about surfing, his eyes were the colour of the sea.

'It used to be like that on the Surfwall,' he said. 'We'd have our backs to the surf, but we could tell by the rhythm of the swells and the sound of the waves when the big one would come. They'd start breaking higher and higher over the wall and most of the blokes would peel off, some of them knew they couldn't hang on. Or they were just plain scared. But not me and Stuart ...'

144

In the second year, just before Easter, she came home for a funeral.

Some of them knew they couldn't hang on, he'd said, *but not me and Stuart – we were the best.* Except that time.

'Fucking stupid. We hadn't even been near the bloody wall for ages – just had to do it one more time – King Tides. And that storm.'

It was almost another cyclone. There hadn't been any real waves, he said, just this huge brown frothy mass of pounding sea. Stuart lost his grip. Got sucked under and then thrown back onto the rocks. 'I almost had him,' he said, 'then another surge came. I couldn't hold on to him and the wall. I had to - I couldn't … I let go.' Apparently it wasn't even safe for any rescue boats to go out, but Stu's body was washed up past South Headland at 11.20 the next day.

When the adults had found out what they'd been doing, and that kids had been doing it on dares for ages, everyone was horrified.

There were front-page stories in the *Gazette*, Mum said, outraged letters to the editor. Speeches at assembly from the headmaster, forbidding anyone ever to go near the Surfwall, whether they were there for school swimming, or in fact at any time. People even talked about electric fences, she said, and some of the public wanted the pool closed, but that didn't happen. They just concreted up a few more rows of bricks then fenced the top with wire netting and barbed wire.

All through school people forgave Danny. For whatever he might have done or had probably dared someone else to do. She could even remember thinking he was a bit of a drip, but really cute. He was always wagging school, forgetting homework, and he was never going to pick up dux of the school or anything, but he became a sort of hero. The football team would have been useless without him, and he'd rescued so many little kids in the surf over the years that parents and teachers thought he was wonderful. All the girls had crushes on him.

But no one looked comfortable at the funeral.

She knew most of the people there, but they weren't really friends. Danny's clothes looked too tight. A few people said 'sorry mate', but even when they were saying it, you could see they blamed him.

'I'm going back to Sydney tomorrow,' she said. 'I've got Dad's car for a while. Come out to Rocky Point with me.'

It was just about her all-time favourite place, Rocky Point.

Walking up to the lighthouse through all those changing colours and textures, you moved past the white sand and that great stretch of tumbled basalt at the base of the cliff, into the shade of the casuarinas and you came through onto on a cool carpet of pine needles. Then the sand became powdery, like ochre dust, darkening to orange brown as you climbed. For a while you could only hear the ocean, then the trees thinned out and the sand hardened into red clay, and suddenly you broke out from that hot, quiet path and there was only clean, salty wind, tufty grass under your feet, and the spiky silhouettes of Pandanus palms leaning out from the top of the headland.

White fountains of spray broke against the columns of the causeway, gulls wheeled and dived, gannets floated on wind currents and you knew you were standing on the edge of a country. Right in a spot that Captain Cook looked at, all those years ago.

It was where she learned nearly all of *The Ancient Mariner*, in the shade of the lighthouse; thought about Danny. What it might be like to go out with him. Cool Danny Johnson.

She spread her arms out wide, felt as though the wind was blowing right through her, as though she was soaking up all that cold, fresh sea air. 'This is where I did my first oil painting,' she told him.

He was still wearing his funeral shoes.

'On-shore wind,' he said. 'piss weak surf.'

146

Part Six

Making a living

"A life of ease is a difficult pursuit."

William Cowper

Booralla, December 1960

MARGARET

A BIT LIKE fishing, this drive. Time to relax. Put the snakes and the storms and the lousy market prices and the ruined frangipanis, and what will we do if he doesn't get this job to the back of her mind. For now anyway. Good straight road, nice breeze with the windows down. At least while they're moving the heat doesn't seem so bad. Cathy making up silly jokes from number plates, pointing out birds and tractors to Nicky who's happy to gaze out the window. Not missing his pillow – yet. The Little Pillow! Not a good start leaving that behind. Hard enough usually getting it off him when it needs washing, impossible to leave it on the line long enough to dry. Well thank god for the road to Booralla scenery. He's obviously content with that for the moment, as she is.

It's always different. More storms forecast later in the week but the sky today almost cloudless. That hot deep blue she'd never seen till they came up here. Mt. Warning clear and dark in the distance, the Poincianas along the river, almost electric green and coming into bloom. Before too long they'll be feathery scarlet umbrellas spaced along the banks. Reminds her of why she's glad to call the place home, in spite of everything. At least now she's got her license – there's going to be a bit of running around if Rob does get the job. Tom and Cathy with swimming lessons, and Nita Carmichael's been at her for weeks to play golf.

She nearly didn't get it – the license ... *Don't be ridiculous; of course you can do it!* She'd been learning for ages and knew how to do it all ... *You're the one complaining about being stuck at the farm ...*

but the thought of going for the test – bad enough Rob's eyes on every gear change and hand signal, she knew that if someone else was watching, her feet and hands wouldn't work at all. But he just pulled up outside the Police Station one day and said he'd booked her in. No time to panic. She knew the Road Rules questions back to front anyway. A turn round the block, up Cemetery Hill, back to the Station and that was it. God, all those excruciating hill-start sessions and reverse parallel-park attempts ...*Gently, gently ... Hand brake! ...Accelerate – now! Turn the wheel – right, not left - right, RIGHT!* Well, with a bit of luck she'd never have to do a reverse parallel again. Then she drove round to The Kalinga Meat Emporium in Beach Street and backed into a light pole. Sobering enough to make her forgive Rob his annoyingly casual congratulations ... *See, nothing to it! Good on you love* ... and turn her into a good, if cautious driver.

He's usually right. Practical Pig his brothers called him and it's perfect. Always cooking up unique solutions to problems. Anyone else would have called in an expert, but he's considered all the angles and can manage by himself thanks very much. The farm won though.

For months the classifieds have been full of dairy farms just about being given away. Now it's bananas. 'Good year,' said the B.G.F. 'good quality, even spread throughout the year, optimum seasonal conditions', so what happens but overproduction. And what was it the Melbourne handlers said? 'Market prices will ease substantially.' She can think of a few other words, and none of them have much to do with ease. 'If growers insist on sending forward fruit' – Rob would never have dreamt of sending them down too ripe. Always kept up with the latest developments, dipping to stop "wet end" and bunchy top, cluster-packing hands loosely in the new, waxed cartons. He was even tempted by the new promotional ideas, but who on earth was going to pay two shillings for a can of mashed banana? And dried ones hadn't exactly caused a stampede.

149

He has to get this job. At least there'll be a regular income. They might even be able to save. On the other hand, God alone knows when the new house will ever get finished. Started if it comes to that. Well, all right, there's a concrete slab lurking there under the lantana, with a beautiful view and a row of stumps that were fran-gipanis till the cows saw more fresh green shoots. And she'll need to put in more time in the shed if he's not around through the day. She's tired. Tired of everything. Snakes in the bathroom, the humidi-ty, the eternal threat of cyclones, mosquitoes, chopping wood, being stuck in that patched-together house. Can't protect the kids from whatever the outside world might throw at them but at least they should be safe at home. How many times has she made excuses when his or her family talk about coming up to sunny Queensland for a holiday – *It's not Queensland, we're on the border but still in New South Wales* – why does Queensland sound more exotic to them? She'd rather die than have them see how they're really living. After three months on the road she'd have swapped the caravan for a packing case. With a bathroom.

Well, she'd got a packing case of sorts – a peeling timber box with jagged gaps in the flaps of corrugated iron that would once have been a roof, and whole rooms – sleep-outs in every sense – with no floorboards. The tank a rusted skeleton, balanced, like the house, on stumps capped with metal discs that the white ants had used as a leg-up. Comfy shelter for a giant carpet snake. *Welcome to your new home … Well I guess it'll be cool …* Rob had christened it "Malua", Fijian for "go gently – do not be in a hurry" … *she'll be right … get it fixed up in no time … start a proper one as soon as we're set* … well that was eight years ago but who's counting. The roof was fixed – after the cyclone – and the floors done. More of Rob's pains-taking home-carpentry, but beautiful in the end, polished wood and all second hand from the sawmill. Not the bathroom though – no need for a proper ceiling or four walls – what's the Fijian word for "never". The ship's never going to come in that far. And since Rob insists on doing everything himself – subtext there being that no one else is going to do the job properly …

Where the hell is he? Said he'd be finished by four and it's nearly half past already. Tom's lesson'll be over – *It's the first day without kickboards. I HAVE to go!* – but Susan's probably glad of the extra time to even up her tan in the new two-piece. Cathy wishing she'd gone to the pool after all. *Can I come with you and Dad? All we ever do is dead man's float and Mr. Johnson spends all day with the little kids.* She wouldn't mind being afloat somewhere. 93 degrees yesterday – hottest day so far, but today feels worse. And it's only the start of December. The heat has melted Nick's good humour, his grizzles now a full-throated tragedy. He's obviously not interested in counting the bees on his playsuit or having his juice cup picked up again. 'Stop annoying him, Cathy.'

'I'm only trying to cheer him up.'

'Maybe you could run round to the newsagent's and get him a little book or something. Get yourself an ice block too. God knows what's happened to your father.'

But *The Little Red Engine* is a dead loss. It's joined his mug on the floor. 'Look Nicky – train', and he's diverted, briefly. Stops sobbing long enough to flip through it, but it doesn't pass muster. Contempt flashing through the hiccups. 'Not much pages.' Which is enough to set Cathy off. "Catherine's marks are good, but could be much better with less giggling in class."

151

CATHY

HE'S TOO HOT but we can't go to the park, Dad should be back any minute. I knew the book wouldn't be any good. We should have brought his P.I.L.L.O.W. but it's not my fault, we all forgot. His little black curls all sweaty and stuck to his head like a Roman soldier. Wet eyelashes, olive skin all flushed. Should have been a girl people say to Mum. We're all hot. He'll be all right but he won't go to sleep without the Little Pillow even though he can hardly keep his eyes open. I shouldn't have laughed but you couldn't beat that could you – "Not much pages" – it only made him crankier and he hardly ever gets cranky, except when you try to cuddle him too much, and it's too hot for cuddles anyway. Even swimming lessons would have been better, but I'm getting proper Speedos for Christmas. Those dumb bloomery things look really stupid when they get wet. And this rotten stuff on the back seat. Feels like the backs of your legs are peeling off when you go to get out, skirt all damp and crushed. I bet real car seats wouldn't be so bad.

It's just that the car's another one of those things Dad made himself. Customized. All of us really excited – Wow a new Holden, two-toned! Then he bought this. Didn't cost as much as a proper Station Wagon, it was a Panel Van, because we need the room if we all go out in the car as well as being able to carry farm things. Then he cut up the floor in the back and made this seat that folds up and down and covered it with dark red vinyl that's meant to look like leather with black lines through it and that sort of crinkly surface. Tom's always finding bits round the edge that he can peel up to make holes in the foam rubber underneath. But there aren't any other doors except the front seat doors, so we all have to climb in which is awful when you're properly dressed and it makes it hotter and there's always sand from last time we went to the beach or spilt chook pellets and the smell of fertilizer.

Not many people could have done it though I s'pose. I mean Dad's not even a real mechanic. Our lowboy too, all fixed and painted with Thumper and Mickey Mouse on each door, people always asking him to do one for their kids. But it's like the house and the bathroom and the hot water system and everything. It takes so long because it all has to be right and there's always so much work to keep the crops going. So some things never get finished. Not enough laminex left over after the kitchen for the last bathroom wall and you had to buy too much just for that and What's the point, we'll be starting the new house soon and it's not as if you can't use the bathroom as it is and for god's sake, who cares what other people think, it's none of their business. But Mum's not talking about the bathroom again. Tom said Steven told his mother that the Williams's haven't even got a proper bathroom and she told some of the ladies at the Tuck shop. And then there was the carpet snake in the rafters the other night when I got out of the shower. It's funny how sometimes you don't think you've said anything but you get such a fright that a scream comes out anyway. That's the dizzy limit Mum said, what if it'd been on the floor and she stepped on it? And Dad said you know they're harmless, they're more scared of us than we are of them, but she just looked at him.

So I've been keeping the bathroom really clean – when I get in there that is, Susan spends so much time making herself beautiful. I keep the taps polished with Brasso and even scrub out the concrete. If all the nice bits, the light green walls and the dark green floor and everything are clean and shiny you don't notice the roof lining through the rafters or the back of the slow combustion stove behind the gap where the toilet would be. Well not so much anyway. I don't have friends out to stay for the weekend much because we don't really have any spare beds and it's a bit far out of town so we can't go to the beach or the pictures all the time, so I really hope he gets this job so there'll be more money and the ship will come in (ha-ha) and they really can get on with the new house.

It'll be terrific to have a toilet inside and not have to chop wood all the time.

MARGARET

NOW NICKY'S HOWLING again and she feels like joining him.

This is ridiculous. If they'd known Rob would be this long she could've brought togs and taken the kids round to the Booralla pool. It'd better be good news after all this. If he says anything about bread on the table or wolves at the door or ships coming in, she'll get back in the driver's seat and run the car into the brick wall with its painted lettering: T W Carmichael & Sons Seed Merchants since 1920 – all she's had to read for the last unbearable, hot sweaty hour. Should have asked Cathy to get a *Women's Weekly*. Must keep up.

She smiles remembering those suits she and her sister had made with their first pay packets. Skirts almost up to the knee, but both of them with legs like Betty Grable and stockings from Carmel's Yankee soldier. Always made a few heads turn on George Street. Golly, was it only fifteen years ago? Rolled hair and nipped waists. When she sees the photo now it seems like a different person. Well they'd caught their men. Carmel in a big house in California. And Margaret. A farmer's wife. You make your bed they'd say and of course she had but he wasn't a farmer then. Ex-air force and so handsome. A commercial artist and making a perfectly good living if you asked her. Business dinners, card parties, quite the high life. And he'd hated it. All the backstabbing and the wheeling and dealing.

So here they are in the Promised Land. Tomatoes, bananas, beans, pineapples, avocadoes, even peanuts. They've tried every crop for every season and she's packed and picked them all and lived through the first six years with two babies a miscarriage and no electricity. Cows too. Never milkers thank god, she couldn't have borne that. Just garden-eating Herefords. And now they've got

Harry in share-farming and Rob's got to give up the dream of being his own boss and *we've got to make a living somehow.*

Don't talk about dreams. Pale green watered silk. The last time she really felt glamorous. One of the advertising do's that had doubled as Rob's farewell. Butterick Evening Patterns. Long skirt, cut glass buttons, burgundy velvet sash. Little black velvet bolero too. A few adjustments on the machine and it was just the thing for Susan at the Fancy Dress Ball. Only a couple of years after they came up that would've been but it was a shame to see the dress go to waste in a tea chest. And Susan now, home from college, quite a knockout. Full of abstract art and jazz. And some lovely outfits. Really smart. Margaret wipes her hands on her seersucker shorts. Myers' country sale. Sydney sounds like a place she doesn't know anymore.

'Hooray', says Cathy and here comes Rob, finally, looking a bit sheepish as well he might, but Margaret can tell from his face that he's got it, and all the anxiety and the festering irritations are washed through with relief and a rush of tenderness that almost makes her cry. She knows she's not the only one who's tired.

Nicky retrieves his little cloth book, 'Look Dad, red engine – red engine book!' 'You're a lucky little bloke aren't you,' says Rob, sliding in behind the wheel.

'Guess what he said when he saw it, Dad?'

'Cathy, don't start that again'.

'Sorry it took so long love, but great news. I start in January. Sales, and actually going out to the farms, so there's a four-wheel drive as well. And we can get the cabin. I've booked two weeks after Christmas.'

… The house at Rocky Point. Fourteen lovely days. Floating in the water, lying on the sand. Electric stove, no fires to light. Reading, fishing.

Nicky is blowing bubbles in the back seat, the car gathers speed and heads east, over the bridge and out of the pressure cooker that is Booralla in summer. Poor Rob, she thinks, who'd want to work there. She leans her head back, lifts the collar off her neck, feels the dampness prickle, then dry. It's always much cooler at home too, lovely on the verandah at this time of the afternoon, under the jacarandas, before the mozzies start. A long cold beer for both of them, to celebrate, and a cigarette, for her – first one for the day, which is good going ...

Rocky Point, Christmas 1961

TOM

SUSAN TOLD HIM that the ship coming in means money, not a real ship. And he knows that the money comes from working. Which is why his father's gone out to the shed again this morning. At first he thought if Dad didn't stay at the beach all the time he'd never see their ship when it did come in, but he said We'll know, don't you worry about it sport.

And Dad always asks him Don't you want to come out to the farm today, but although he still goes up to the shed sometimes to help Harry packing, it's not like it used to be when Mum and Cathy and Dad were all there, singing the Banana Boat song, or Hang Down your Head Tom Dooley. Or Cathy doing silly singing like the Chipmunks. Dad only whistled, because if he tried to sing everybody just laughed. Even Harry. The smells are different now too. Banana sap that makes your hands all black and sticky and cardboard cartons mostly, or avocadoes that don't really have any smell you remember, instead of green beans and furry tomato stalks and stencil ink for the bean bags and packing cases. And those little hills of bad tomatoes that got thrown out for the cows, turning sloppy in the sun. The cows would just slosh through the pile outside and poke their heads in the shed looking for the nice ones that were going to market.

Now that the girls are on holidays, instead of away at college or teaching or in high school, he'd rather stay out at the beach. He can play with them, because they're not so little that it's dangerous to do anything, like another certain person he can think of. There's too many things he can't do when Nicholas is there. Everyone's always afraid he'll drown or tread on a toadfish or something. Or Mum will say Let him help you with the sand castle, and Nicholas tries to do it with sand that's too dry or too wet. Or if Tom's made a really good one, Nicholas treads on the special battlements. On purpose. And he can't swim yet, so everyone has to watch what he's doing. Nicholas that is. Tom can. Well, he could swim properly if there was a pool here like Mr. Johnson's. He nearly can in the creek. If he gets the surfoplane for Christmas he'll be able to ride waves, and Nicholas really is too little to do that.

SUSAN

FUNNY, BUT IT was still hard to imagine actually telling Mum and Dad that she might not come home for Christmas next year. Just how to broach the subject without feeling as though she was breaking some sort of unspoken family rule. She'd already invited Jane to come and spend the fortnight at Rocky Point over Christmas this year. She hardly ever saw any of the girls from school that she used to hang around with. If they did come back from wherever they'd gone away to, it was usually with boyfriends. At least when Jane came there'd be something to do, someone to go out with at night. Someone who knew there were things going on in the world outside Kalinga.

Maybe they could go to some of the surf club dances, or the pictures. Susan knew most of the surf club boys by now, and these days, a lot of them weren't locals anyway. They came down from Brisbane on weekends through the year, and in the Christmas holidays they got bed and board in return for doing the beach patrols.

Jane's parents had asked her out to stay at their property over the September break. She'd got on really well with the family – her brother was very dishy – and they'd said it would be lovely if she could go there for Christmas next year. They'd say something when Jane came up, Susan thought; Mum and Dad wouldn't be able to say no while Jane was there. Well, why would they anyway, but at least with Jane there, she mightn't feel so guilty.

It had been odd staying on the Whitworth's sheep station though. Horses everywhere, so she'd actually been living out the dream she'd had all those years ago; but there was always so much dusty wind and so many flies it was almost dangerous to open your mouth. She'd hated the idea that you could ride for miles and miles and the mountains just seemed to get further away. Mountains blocking the horizon where the sea should be, and nothing but flat land to the west; it was like being hemmed in somehow, by all that space.

As soon as she got off the bus in Kalinga, Tom said, 'My swimming is really good now. I can swim by myself. Can I have a coddle?'

'You mean a cuddle,' she said, and gave him a big hug, 'you're getting tall now, aren't you?'

'Nicholas can't even do the dog paddle properly,' he said. 'I might be getting a Coolite board for Christmas.'

He seemed to be pretty sure about who Santa Claus was these days, but he'd been sworn to secrecy so Nicky wouldn't find out. Tom still didn't know for sure if he *was* getting the board for Christmas, but it managed to get a mention every time Nicky happened to be within earshot. Along with broad hints that telling Mum and Dad what he wanted was a more likely way of getting presents than writing a letter to the North Pole.

Susan can't actually remember ever suddenly having to accept that all the grownups had been telling her fibs about someone with a big tummy and a red suit, who didn't exist. Come to think of it, she can't really remember anyone actually telling her about Father Christmas. But it had to be pretty puzzling for some little kids. The year Tom started kindergarten, he did still expect Santa to find their house, even though they didn't have a street number and he'd have trouble getting down the slow-combustion flue. He'd also been having lots of night-before-Christmas stories at school, and the good old Nativity play on speech night. He was one of the flock watchers, in his flannelette dressing gown. By the time Christmas Eve arrived, he'd got so excited that even though he'd already gone to bed a bit later than normal, he kept tiptoeing out and peering round the door to the living room hoping he'd catch Santa putting presents under the tree. Maybe share a glass of milk and a couple of Ginger Nuts.

After the third appearance, even Cathy had gone to bed, and Susan was ready to. Mum and Dad were getting a bit impatient because they were trying to wrap all the goodies. The fourth time, after a mad scramble to hide everything, Dad was more than impatient. 'Once more, Tom,' he'd said, in a tone that would have stopped most people, 'if I see you out here once more, it will be smacks. No Father Christmas and no presents. For anybody!'

Tom was getting a bit teary by then, but he stood his ground and braved one final comeback. 'Anyway,' he said, bottom lip quivering, 'I hate Father Christmas.' And seconds later, from the kitchen, 'and I hate the baby Jesus!'

Next morning all was forgiven. But if it wasn't, he was able to get it off his chest by blasting everyone in sight with his new cap gun, and it didn't really matter who'd delivered it.

MARGARET

THE SOUTHERLY IS coming in, drifts curling through the sleepy afternoon. She can hear the she-oaks stir at her back; the cool slap of the estuary water on the wall below, catch the momentary flash, flick and ripple from the odd jumping mullet. From the beach side of the far bank come the echoes of laughter and thrilled squeals from Tom as the girls repeatedly set him up and launch him from the top of the dunes in his cardboard box toboggan.

She's had no bites all afternoon, but it doesn't matter. She wouldn't eat mullet in a fit, and they will have chased any bream or whiting away. She lets the tide pull lazily at the line, untangles the occasional snag from the oyster-shelled rocks and is lulled by the peace, by Nicky's warm little body leaning into hers.

There's no choice – even she has to admit that. If it gets down to the holiday at the beach or a bit more money set to aside for the new house, she'll always choose the holiday. Especially now that their income is not dependent on the whims of the weather and plant life. Even though most days, Rob still ducks out to the farm for a couple for hours or so, to do some bookkeeping that he didn't want to bring to the beach – or she wouldn't let him bring to the beach – to give Harry a hand or simply check that everything's ok, he's much more relaxed.

He'll have all the December ledgers tied up by Christmas, has promised he'll spend as much time as possible helping Tom learn how to use the board. Tom's going well with his swimming, but he's still a bit intimidated when the waves are dumpy close in to shore. She was horrified when Rob's original reaction to swimming lessons, half teasing or not, had been *just throw him in, he'll soon work out how to stay afloat. That's how we all learned*. Not unlike his response when she'd been so outraged by the idea of that dreadful Murray woman at school trying to bully Tom, and presumably other children, out of left handedness: *If you want to go up to the school and complain, go ahead. I can't see that it's worth such a song and dance. We can't be coddling the boy all the time. Things would probably be worse for him if we did make a fuss.*

Well, he may have been right, but she's glad Tom's away from Mrs. Murray's clutches at last. And his nightmares seem to have eased off. There certainly haven't been any sleepwalking episodes for quite a while.

And now Christmas is only three days away, but she's actually looking forward to it. They'll all be here for Christmas dinner – well, just the immediate family, and Jane, which is fine by her. When she thinks what would be going on in Parry Street now. Or even if they were back at the farm.

How many times has she been in the kitchen on what inevitably turns out to be either the wettest or the hottest day of the year – all right, that's probably an exaggeration, and she's sure Rob would have the rainfall and temperature figures available somewhere – but no matter what the weather, she'd be the one wrestling a stuffed turkey with all the trimmings, the temperamental oven. There are always plenty of offers to help, Cathy and Susan love decorating the tree, wrapping presents, setting the table with all its once a year finery, but she's done the meal itself for so many years now, it's a routine, mapped out in her head and easier if she does it herself – too many cooks and all that. Year before last though, actually the year of the 'baby Jesus', she'd come close to resigning her post before she'd finished stuffing the turkey. Someone was silly enough to send Tom a little drum and a set of sticks. What with that as well as the cowboy hat and cap gun he'd been begging for all year, they'd had to make him put it all away till later or at least go as far down the other end of the yard as possible. Which all added to the drama.

164

MAKING A LIVING

But she always does it, the 'traditional' dinner, because even though she's often too weary to eat or enjoy any of it by the time she sits down, the rest of the family would be horrified at the thought of Christmas day without the feast. Without the wishbones, and the bonbons and the turkey stuffing. And it is a chance to break out some of the special crockery, the damask linen, cut glass dishes and good cutlery, the ornate silver nutcracker, all the accoutrements for polite dining that followed them up from Melbourne and rarely see the light of day. Even their new house, whenever it does materialize into something more substantial than Rob's sketches, is unlikely to have the sort of interior décor that will sport a glass-fronted china cabinet.

The beauty of being at the beach is that no one seems to mind cold meat. She prepared the ham and turkey before they came out to Rocky Point – was able to select a reasonably mild day to do it. And as long as there are plenty of the festive additions, goodies they never eat at any other time in summer – well, hardly ever if she thinks about it – the cranberry sauce, the plum pudding with brandy custard and plenty of well-apportioned sixpences, the one surprise shilling, the fruit cake in its frilled tinsel jacket, licorice all sorts, mince pies. And the nuts: every type of nut, to crack with the silver nutcracker. Walnuts are always good, easy to extricate whole; hazel nuts a bit more of a challenge; brazils very difficult, but worth the effort, mashed or not. And then there are the macadamias. Or macedonians, macadanians, depending on which of the children is discussing them, sugar bags full from the Robinson's tree every year. The only way to expose their secret heart is to take a hammer to them on the concrete. Whoever can open the most without breaking the kernel also gets to eat the most. So every year, one or two more cracks appear in the path to the back door. If she could only harness the energy with which the kids are happy to sit at this task for days at Christmas time. Instead, for the rest of the year, discarded, too

165

hard nuts sit at the bottom of the fruit bowl, can be heard rolling around in unlikely places, lurk with the dust balls under beds and behind couches, or simply disappear altogether.

There probably wouldn't have been any nuts left to disappear at Parry St. And they'd usually all been shelled by whichever child had been given that job a week beforehand, lots roasted by her mother at midnight or some ungodly hour that she was still in the kitchen with just one more thing she wanted to do before she went to bed. Heavens above, all the chopping, mincing, baking and roasting that used to start weeks before Christmas day; her mother preparing the annual feast for at least the ten in their family, and more often than not various uncles, aunts and cousins who called around for a bit of Christmas cheer, to drop off presents and would end up staying for cups of tea that extended into *well, I wouldn't say no to a bite to eat, that cake looks delicious,* and eventually – *stay for lunch, come on, you need a bit more meat on those bones - there's enough for ten, what's a few more.*

Whenever she pictures Ma, it's always with an apron on, in the kitchen, pegging out the washing, talking to the neighbours over the side fence. Otherwise she's in the hat and coat, going to Mass, funerals, christenings, weddings, off on the tram into town or the Ashgrove butchery, green grocer. There'd be marathon card games, their mother still in and out of the kitchen, whipping up the odd batch of scones in the time it took most people to extend or accept the invitation to stay on for tea. Laying another place at the table so the boys could eat first, get off to cricket practice or the pictures or whatever they might have lined up. Then the littlies could eat together, be ready for bed or go out to play until it got dark.

New house or not, there are aspects of life at McClaren's Ridge that she knows are enviable, and for which she is grateful. One guest is plenty.

She'll have to remember to ask Norma for some bedclothes so Cathy can use the divan. She said she's looking forward to sleeping in the living room – *I'll be able to smell the Christmas tree all night.* They all went for a walk along the creek in the cool of the afternoon yesterday, and selected a small, perfectly shaped she-oak. Just need to search for some decently sized rocks to anchor it in the bucket Rob's bringing back, along with the tomahawk. The girls can decorate it tomorrow.

She won't be surprised if this is the last time they'll all be home for Christmas every year. She knew when Susan started staying in Sydney for term holidays, or going to Jane's parents' property that the day would not be long in coming. It's not something to be dwelt upon though. Not only is there amazement that the years seem to have disappeared so easily, which certainly makes her feel her age if she broods too long, but Nicky waits in the wings, about to start his journey, which affords little room for self pity or sentimentality. It seems a long time since Susan was a child. And she's always been independent; like Rob.

Cathy has been quieter lately, although she does live in a bit of a dream world – sometimes it's hard to tell what's going on in there.. Probably missing Christine, but she'd never say. And anyone can see she's developed a rather surprising crush on Melvin all of a sudden. Doomed of course, but like all these things, unlikely to last long enough to cause any heartache.

She's glad though that they'll probably be seeing more of Jean and Harold. Well, she'll be glad to see more of Jean, silver spoon or not. Like most of Rob's side of the family, she was decidedly a little forbidding on first meeting, but she's great company, always good for a laugh, ready to call a spade a spade and to share a sherry as soon as the sun's decently over the yardarm. They're already talking about a trip up to the Lamington Park Lodge next year sometime.

CATHY

THE SEA IS just how I like it today, shallow at low tide for a long way out and almost green. Calm, so you can get wet gradually and duck dive when it's getting harder to stand on the bottom, because the water's carrying you onto your tiptoes or the sand starts to slope away. Underwater, your feet can grip all the little ridges in the sand. It looks like ripple soled shoes because the swell is so gentle they haven't been disturbed, and back up where the sand is dry it's all white and fine to walk on, the way it is on the high dunes behind the beach. Climbing up or down there takes ages, because with every step you sink right in and little avalanches bury your feet. Sometimes down here when the storms come from the northeast, the wind whips away that flat soft blanket below the sand hills, and you can see the rutile that they're mining on the beaches further down at Yimbun and Wattle Creek. A glinty black pattern following the wind and tide lines. It always seems to stick to your toes more than the white sand, but maybe that's just because you can see it. Dad says that's why.

We are in the cabin again this year. Everyone calls it the house at Rocky Point, but it is a group of cabins. Each one is sort of divided in half, with a kitchen and living room in one part, then two bedrooms on the other side, one where Mum and Dad sleep, and bunks in the other one for all of us. This year I will sleep on the couch when Jane comes. Susan's best friend from college. There is a main building too, where some people have rooms like in a guest- house and can eat with Norma and Ted who own the flats. I think there are bathrooms in the main house too. We have to go to the laundry block to have showers. It would be nice to have a holiday in a real hotel. I don't think we've ever done that. Maybe when I was little but I don't remember.

The time I went to Sydney to stay with Grandma, Aunty Jean and Uncle Harold had been to a fete at Melvin's school and they were taking him out for lunch, so they arranged to come and pick me up too. They said we were going to a Hotel called The Bay Shore, and I could just imagine having tea and sandwiches like the ladies you'd see in the English pictures, with high heels and parasols, sitting on a big cool verandah with palm trees in pots.

We drove down the Bay Road all along the cliff tops, with the sea on one side and big white houses, lovely green lawns, pine trees and seagulls blowing in the sky. I only had sandals on, but I still felt like one of those grand ladies. When we got out of the car, all our shoes crunched on the gravel path that led up to the front doors, and there were big pots at the entrance with dark green hedgey bushes clipped into shapes like balls. Aunty Jean wasn't carrying a parasol, but she was wearing perfume and a floaty dress and she looked very stylish when she smoked cigarettes. There was a little orchestra playing music in the dining room, and the waiter pulled our chairs out for us.

What Melvin and I actually had was fish and chips, but on a plate and with lots of knives and forks. Melvin said I don't know why we couldn't just go and sit outside down at the Jetty. Yes, but you know we like it here dear, Aunty Jean said to him, your father particularly, and the Thermidor is always so good. There were special little glass cruets for the salt and pepper, vinegar if you wanted that, tiny jugs of tartare sauce and silver tongs to pick up the lemon slices. All the table-cloths and serviettes were like our really good white ones. It was a bit like having fish and chips for Christmas dinner. Afterwards they wheeled a silver trolley around to the table with so many different sorts of cakes and deserts I nearly ended up not having anything because I got embarrassed about taking so long to decide.

It was all lovely and I couldn't wait to tell Susan about it when I got home. She probably goes to places like that all the time now. Melvin acted as if it was just an ordinary day. I didn't like him then, but maybe now that we get along all right we could go there next time I visit Sydney.

But, for now, it's still the other way round. Christmas pudding and custard, bare feet and sand on the floor. And the smell of she-oaks.

Part Seven

Leaving 2

McClaren's Ridge, October 1964

CATHY

'IF YOU KNEW all your chemistry as well as you know all the words to the Hit Parade, you'd be top of the class.'

Dad thinks Roy Orbison's dreadful. He always used to drive Susan mad too, when she liked Buddy Holly and he'd sing *Peggy Sue* in this stupid voice just to tease her, because he can't sing for nuts.

I'm sitting on the back step trying to get my legs brown, summarizing different topics I know we'll get questions about in Geography onto little pieces of paper with points one to whatever so I can remember how many points in each topic and learn those to expand on. Well it usually works. And singing along to *Pretty Woman*. I'll pass Geography anyway, but Maths and Science are the problem. Which is something that drives *Dad* mad. He tries to help but he can't see how I could possibly get the answers I do after a page of algebra calculation, when he can get a pretty good idea of what the answer should be just by looking at the question.

Anyway, I don't really want to pass. Well, that's not true. I don't want to fail, but I'm younger than most of the kids in our class, so if I had to do the Leaving Certificate again I wouldn't care. I like going away for holidays, but if I pass and get good enough marks to go to Uni it'll be the beginning of going away forever.

Melvin really doesn't care if he passes or not.

'I'm getting out as soon as I've finished,' he said. 'Why don't you come with me?'

'Don't be mad,' I said, 'how can I? Where will you go?'

'Over the mountains,' he said, 'across the ocean, who knows – there's lots of jungles and rope bridges out there. I might even take my binoculars.'

All right for some people. Anyway he's got to be joking. God, Mum and Dad would kill me.

November 1958

SUSAN

WELL, MIRACLES DID happen. She was finally able to finish the Miser-ables. Under the light of her new bed lamp. And it was so much easier to read the tiny print. Trying to read it before was impossible unless it was daylight. And reading Mrs. Elliot's copy had turned out to be a bit like the *Arthur Mee's Encylopedias*. She'd got to the end and discovered the last two chapters were missing. But then, *Les Miserables* was on their Leaving Certificate booklist, so she made sure to check that it said The End on the back page before she picked her copy off the textbook pile.

Tom wasn't excited about the "lectriclines" anymore. He kept asking her 'Why do you have to go away? Can't you study here?' They'd had to stop reading *Winnie the Pooh* before the "Enchanted Place" chapter. His lips always started to tremble when it came to the last verse of *The Teddy Bears' Picnic*. Sometimes the way he yelled out in the night was enough to curdle your blood, but most of the time he didn't actually wake up.

She was leaving though. Only a few months to go before she turned into Susan Williams, teacher trainee. And if she didn't ask a certain person to the School Leaving party today, it would be too late.

It was the sort of weather where the effort of drying yourself af-ter a shower left you wetter than before. That heat that waited till just after the exams. It was always the same, but it always seemed worse than it was the year before. You'd get these great heavy piles of cloud hanging low all day in the west, and the Border Ranges were just like a hazy smudge. Even the blue space between the sea horizon and its sort of pink cumulus frieze looked pale and washed out.

She needed to get wet. Little itchy trickles of coconut oil were sidling down her neck and stomach. The best thing was just to lie in the shallow lagoon between the sand spit and the ocean, and when that got too much like a warm bath, dive into the surf, sun bake dry, then go out again.

But Danny was out there. When the lifesavers all went past with their skis, he'd smiled at her and said 'Hi', so she had to stay put. At least till he came out.

She pushed her shoulder straps down and rolled over, facing the surf, to toast her back. Let the towel soak up the TanFast and perspiration. Which made her feel a bit like a rock lizard, propped up on her elbows. But that way, if she half closed her eyes, she could watch them. Sleek golden heads and shoulders, like glistening seals they were, lined up out there in the sunlight. Most of them were Surfwall boys. And the ones that weren't wished they were. But that was up to Danny. He pretty much owned the Surfwall.

They didn't do it much anymore. Grown out of it partly. Once in a while you'd still see a bunch of younger kids huddled together over on the far side of the pool. Watching the swells and checking to see if anyone was looking. But they never got much further than crouching on the edge to jump, before Danny's father would come steaming out of his little kiosk yelling blue murder. 'Get away from there, you young larrikins! G'on, get out, or youse'll get what ya deserve.'

Danny and his mates had got crazy about surfboard riding now. Last year, he and Stuart Cooper had gone to Long Reef for the first National Championships, and now it was all they talked about. They were out there now, pretending their wave skis were Malibus.

175

A lot of the older club members were saying they'd turned into lairs – bleaching their hair, more interested in finding a good wave than saving people. Surfboards were a danger to little kids and serious body surfers they reckoned. Just jealous, according to Danny.

But they were still the ones who took all the risks – still the ones always furthest out. There wasn't one of them who couldn't out-swim everyone else in Kalinga, and none of them could out-swim Danny. Hair just a bit longer and blonder than all the others, shoulders a bit wider. He moved like the water. He wasn't always the first one to catch a wave – he was picky - but when he did go, he was the one everybody watched. Well, Susan did too, but Yvonne's brother reckoned he'd been looking in her direction lately too. Definitely taking notice, anyway.

'Susan's got a crush on Danny Johnson.' Cathy, being her usual annoying self. 'Joyce and Shorty's boy?' Mum said, 'I thought he'd left school.' He had, but 'He's working with his Dad,' Susan said – which he was supposed to be. But she didn't care anyway. All the boys in her class were absolute creeps; she couldn't stand the thought of going to the break up party with any of them. And after the holidays she'd be going to college.

Then, there he was, standing between her and the sun, shaking his hair like a wet puppy. And the chill of those droplets spraying onto her burning skin made her toes tingle. 'Hey doll,' he said, 'how's it going?' The other boys had gone on, and even though she knew Yvonne and Barbara were watching every move from back near the Pavilion, it felt as though there was no one else on the beach.

They talked a bit about everyday things; what people were going to do next year, how he and Stuart wanted to travel, surf other beaches, how, maybe, they might go out sometime. Together. She leapt in then with both feet and asked about the farewell party.

176

'That'd be cool', he said, and smiled in that way he had, like a sleepy lion. He already had his license too, so he could pick her up in his Dad's car.

So for the rest of the holidays she was famous for being Danny's girlfriend. All the girls in her class were green with envy, a bit awed that she'd actually dared to ask him. Mum wasn't that impressed, but because Susan would soon be going away, she wasn't saying too much. Dad seemed to think it was the end of the world, but Susan said 'Well, I'll be in Sydney next year – I could be going out all the time – with anybody'.

He and his mates did drink a fair bit, but not so much when it was just her and Danny. At least he'd stopped saying things like 'Fancy me going out with a brainy sheila like you.' 'Don't be stupid,' she'd told him. 'That's a silly thing to say.'

But Susan was in a dream world. Just being close enough to touch those smooth brown hands, looking back into those blue green eyes, she was happy to drown, or floating round the house, doing ordinary things, washing up, making the bed, looking in the mirror, she would suddenly feel giddy just thinking about him, realising that at that precise moment he could be thinking about her too – it was like her own electric charge.

December 1967

TOM

HE JUST WANTS to get away. Susan's been gone so long he forgets what she looks like half the time. Cathy comes home and moons about, goes for long walks by herself, or sits in the sun drying her hair with these huge rollers like hairy caterpillars all over the back of her head and scotch tape across her fringe. Otherwise she listens to records in her bedroom – not with candles anymore – 'It took long enough to get this house built,' Dad said, 'don't burn it down before the paint dries.'

Every time she brings her college stuff home there's another bottle to add to the collection of those ones with the straw jackets and coloured wax all artily dribbled down the side. Then she leaves half of them here because her bags are already too full to take them back. He'd have thrown Percy Sledge out with the compost accidentally on purpose if he'd had to listen to *that* record once more. Now she's working on making everyone sick of hearing about Billy Joe McAllister jumping off a bridge with a name nobody can pronounce properly. And the idea of going to San Francisco with flowers in your hair –she didn't even want to go to Uni at first.

Some of the records she's got you never hear – not at home anyway – Sgt Pepper, Jefferson Airplane, Tim Buckley. He'd bet that she goes on protest marches and smokes too, but she's such a goody-goody she'd never admit that at home. His parents wouldn't want a rebellion on their hands. He can't get through a day now without having a violent disagreement about anything with his father. And Mum can't stand arguments, so it's easier not to talk to any of them.

The war might as well not be happening for all they seem to care. Well, they might care if it's still on when he's old enough to be conscripted. Or maybe not. His father probably thinks going to Vietnam to stem the Red Tide might be the making of him – just what he needs to knock some sense into him. Well, there's always student exemption. He'll get into Uni, it's just a case of which one. Or conscientious objection – that would open an ugly can of worms. He doubts that his parents even know he realizes such a thing exists, let alone that it's what he would do if pushed.

Still, that's all in the future.

But it's a future that can't come soon enough for him, along with an escape from the boredom and narrow mindedness that is life in Kalinga.

January 1965

CATHY

EVERYONE ELSE FINISHED breakfast hours ago. Dad's gone to work, Tom's at cricket practice and Nicky's already off outside somewhere. It's Saturday morning and the Beach Boys are on the radio, reminding me of all the things I'll be leaving. There are big wet splotches all over the page I'm up to in *Death in Venice* and my vegemite toast is getting cold. On the back verandah the twin-tub has stopped spinning and Mum comes in, surprised to see me still in the kitchen. I try to blow my nose quietly. I must look as if I'm wearing clown makeup.

'Oh, Cathy,' she says, 'not again. You'll be okay. Really. It's a wonderful opportunity.'

Well.

The usual question that follows is *What would you do with your life if you stayed here* and there are several answers to that, which are quite satisfactory or very unsatisfactory, depending on who you are telling them to.

Some things happen gradually, so you hardly notice. Then one day you realize something is different and probably always will be.

I mean, Susan went away to college. At first she came home every term, then some holidays she stayed at friends' places, or she'd come back but she'd bring friends with her and mostly spend time with them. When she started teaching she got sent to some place nobody ever heard of, then suddenly she brought Ross home and they were engaged and then they got married last year and I was a bridesmaid and my hair was all teased and stiff and just looked horrible and I cried all through the church and my dress was too long. The picture on the pattern cover looked like what it was meant to – a bell skirt. On me it ended up looking like a tea cosy walking round on two skinny legs. Susan looked perfect. They look a lot like each other actually. Blonde and tan, and they both like jazz and the sorts of energetic outdoor things that involve knowing how to put up a tent and not caring if there isn't any hot water. That's how they got interested in each other. The fact that he's Jane's brother helped too.

Now they live about as far away from Kalinga as you can get and still be in the same state.

And that was all in the same year that Pam and Diane and I went to Brisbane and we met up with Christine and saw *West Side Story*. I wore lipstick and the pointy toed high heels I had for Susan's wedding and a new dress Mum had made with a scoop neck and wide belt that I could pull in tight enough to make it look as though I had a bit more up top and I thought I might look like Patsy Anne Noble. But I cried so much at the end of the film that my face was all puffed up and red and I kept having to blow my nose and wipe my eyes so much on the bus going home that the others got a bit embarrassed after a while.

Then President Kennedy got shot. There was a group of us standing outside Myers. Just after the exams it was, and we heard someone say it had just come over the radio that JFK had been shot in Dallas and might be dead. That was just so awful that at first I didn't cry. Then it was on the television. The worst thing was seeing Jackie trying to hold him up in the car. Then his son at the funeral in that little coat. And every time I heard Joan Baez sing anything, I cried. And the song that we always belted out at the back of the bus on school excursions was *It's My Party (and I'll Cry if I Want To)*.

Things are looming.

I enjoy schoolwork – well, I like illustrating intricate pictures of hieroglyphics and Egyptian mummies, colouring maps, ruling up new exercise books, translating Latin and French grammar, reading, and reading. And I even like exams. As long as there's none of the 'if two men can run twenty miles over four days, how long would it take forty men to walk three feet' sort of thing.

But then there's teaching. It's just something I can't even imagine doing. All those IQ tests haven't shown much except that I would make someone a useful secretary. I do like sharpening pencils and putting things away, but apart from living on a deserted island and reading books, if I have to have a job, all I've ever really wanted to do was be a reporter. That was since I abandoned any hope of becoming a champion swimmer or a prima ballerina. But someone said that you were supposed to leave school after the Intermediate to do a Cadetship. Like all those people who go off to do things like hairdressing or apprenticeships. Leaving school after the Intermediate wasn't actually something Mum and Dad would have taken seriously even if I had been game to bring it up. I would matriculate, I would go to university, and I would become a teacher.

Most of the girls I get around with are headed for the same fate. Well, what else is there, unless you're beautiful like Christine and know people who know people like June Dally Watkins and have a mother that even considers such things as fashion or modelling to be a possible vocation. We can't stay in Kalinga, and we're far too young to be thinking about marriage and babies. That will all take care of itself.

I mean I did study, because I hate doing badly at anything. And I did all right. Plan A worked. I did miss the 'first intake', but now the worst has happened. The Letter came last week. I got in on the second round. Which everyone else, Mum and Dad that is, think is wonderful, and not really a surprise. I just don't want to go.

But I have to admit, I like filling out forms. Even occasionally thinking about what it might be like to live somewhere that actually has seasons other than hot and wet and cool and dry. Choosing course Units is interesting, and studying booklists, and so is organising tickets and reading up about the college, sorting out what clothes to take, and luggage, and making shopping lists, but then I'll think – this is leaving.

Even after I'd opened the letter and I was walking back up the road from the mail box with the hard red mud cool under the soles of my feet, and the smell of honeysuckle coming off the creepers on the cutting, I wondered if that would be the last time I would ever go down to collect the mail. Tom and Nicky usually take turns to do it now, or they race each other down. And every day I wake up and think I'll never really live here again, in this house. I won't be one of the Williams girls going to school here anymore. And even while I realize I'm being really sad and stupid, that makes me cry as well because of how wet and hopeless I am and how could someone like that be any good at university and I should just stay here and plant beans or milk cows and watch the sunset or something and be happy. But would I be?

'Do you want me to help you put the zip in that Mary Quant pattern you were finishing off yesterday?' Mum said.

'That would be good,' I said. 'I want to find some coffee lace too, for the collar on that velvet jacket.'

We went to town later and got some lovely lace, some new underwear, a couple of suspender belts and some black stretch pants. I've actually got enough in the way of a bust now to justify wearing a bra too. Thirty two triple-A, but still.

I sewed in the afternoon and I didn't cry once. I have started telling myself that if I don't go to University I'll never get a job that will pay me enough (even if it does have to be teaching) so that I can save up to go and see Venice. Or the Deep South.

I mean if you want to see the world, you might as well do it properly.

Part Eight

Going back

"O let them be left, the wildness and wet

Long live the weeds and the wilderness yet."

Gerard Manly Hopkins

Kalinga, December 1960

SUSAN

SHE THOUGHT DANNY hadn't seen her, but she could hear Tom saying 'My big sister's home from college, Mr. Johnson, she brought me today,' and before she could get out of sight she got the big wave. Still, she'd rather be at the pool than down in Booralla. It was so hot. Not that she didn't really hope Dad got this job, but they didn't all need to go with him. And Tom hadn't wanted to miss this week's lesson. Plus, she needed to get a bit of colour before she could go public in the new bikini.

Junior swimming classes and bronze medal training. 'Mr. Johnson, Mr. Johnson, watch me!' All the little girls clustered round, dripping and puffing. Danny still had his fan club, only they were getting younger.

Tom was actually the only boy in Danny's swimming class, at least that day, and he was still in the water. Dog-paddling his way across the littlies' pool for the fifth time.

She'd said to him 'Dad's seeing if we can get the house at Rocky Point again. You'd be able to practice swimming every day then,' and he said 'Maybe the ship will be able to come in at Rocky Point.'

She wasn't sure what he meant at first, but then she'd laughed, and he did too, but she could see he didn't mean it as a joke. Poor Tom; used to follow Dad all over the farm, happy as Larry. Now Dad had to get this job at Carmichaels' because the farm wasn't making enough.

'If the ship comes in,' Tom had said, 'then we can make a living, and Dad can come back. And now you've finished college, maybe you could come back.'

'Dad's not going away,' she said, 'if he gets this job he'll just have to go into Booralla through the day and you'd be at school anyway. I don't know where I'll be teaching yet, but I can come home for holidays.'

'You didn't come all this year.'

That was true. Not since last Christmas. Most of her friends were in Sydney now.

Danny had never got his surf shop. Mum said he was too busy with his Dad, trying to keep the pool going, but the Council had been talking about building a big new indoor pool up in Kalinga Heights, so they might even be closing the Headland Pool down. Cathy said it was creepy doing deep-diving for medal training, because of all the green slime on the bottom of the Surfwall pool.

It was meant to be a family thing, the Pool, but there was no sign of Shorty. Apparently his usual routine was hosing out the dressing sheds after breakfast then spending the rest of day propping up the bar at the Golf Club. Watching Joycie flirt with all the men, Mum said. Crying into his beer if he stayed too long – '*my pool, my own bloody son – shoulda known what was going on – did know – shoulda stopped it.*' He hardly spoke to Danny anymore, she said, and when Joycie wasn't tending bar, she was round at Danny's, telling Pam how to bring up the baby.

There was a tail of rusty barbed wire hanging down the surf-wall.

'Can you come and be a teacher at our school,' Tom said, 'in-stead of Mrs. Murray.'

Tom used to be left- handed. 'That bloody woman,' Mum said when she found out about Mrs. Murray. 'Every time he did any-thing with his left hand she hit him with the ruler. Now he just writes badly with both hands!'

187

That'd be Tom, always trying to do the right thing and not game to say anything because Mrs. Murray's made him think left-handed people are evil or something. He was almost drowning as she watched, forgetting to breathe while he showed Danny how well he could kick and how he wasn't afraid to keep his head down.

But Mr. Johnson actually seemed more interested in a certain person's new bikini. Pacing up and down with his whistle and that tan. She thought he was going to offer to help with the coconut oil for a while there. He'd be lucky.

The thing was - being at the beach again was terrific. It was easy to forget what summer really smelled like, red soil steaming in the afternoon rain, salty skin, mangoes, frangipani ...

But she didn't think she could stay in Kalinga – McClaren's Ridge.

Hanging out nappies in the morning and swapping recipes and knitting patterns in the afternoon – that seemed to be the daily routine of most of the girls from school who'd stayed around. Married to boys like Danny Johnson. Wiping down the laminex and emptying the ashtrays and waiting for the Surfwall Boys to come home with their bottles of beer and their big stories.

And the house. She'd forgotten how small it was. Still not finished and Mum still hated it. Embarrassed at having people come to stay. Dad said 'Things will be better when this job at Carmichaels' comes through. We'll get builders to finish off the new house.'

'Why don't you tell Mum you're trying to get the house at Rocky Point for the holidays?' she asked him, after Mum had been so upset about the snake in the bathroom and everything. 'I want it to be a surprise,' he said.

Well, Father's supposed to know best, sometimes you have to pick the right moment to surprise someone.

There are days when she can't wait to get back to Sydney.

McClaren's Ridge, Easter 1965

CATHY

HE'S SHARPENING KNIVES on the whetstone when I go in with Mum. Michael Thompson. He looks up and I start to look away, but he's seen me and he gives a sort of half smile, so I smile at the air above his head – well, at the big white haunch of beef with its red stamp and glistening fat coat on a silver hook above his head – and I'm so nervous it probably looks more like I smelt something nasty. Then I study the footprint patterns in the sawdust on the floor till Mum pays and we're out of the shop. She's not one for getting involved in the sort of jolly butcher conversations about prime cuts and choicest kidneys that some of the ladies love.

And I've pretty well ignored him. This boy that I chose to be my pretend Prince in Kindergarten, to lead the pretend Coronation with our pretend crowns that I'd made. They had little bits of coloured glass glued on from old broken bottles that Susan and I used to find buried under the house. This boy that makes my stomach flip every time I see him. Do I think I'm so good because I'm home from University and he's an apprentice in a butcher's shop? What I really want to ask is does he get enough time to go surfing, does he still draw, why did he choose butchery and how can he stand cutting up all that raw meat.

So I spend the rest of the day feeling odd about being back home and wondering what I'm going to do with myself. Apart from baby-sit of course. Other than get on with *Robbery Under Arms*, while I sun bake in one of Susan's really brief bikinis that she left here last Christmas when she got a new even briefer pair. Eating all the black

jelly beans Mum's been saving for me. And hating myself for looking at the sawdust.

The old shed's been levelled. Because it was too close to where
they had to bulldoze for the new house. Harry's put up a rough
shed over in the back paddock, so he's closer to his family's dairy
farm as well. I hardly ever went to the shed after I got to High
School, even to talk to Harry. The sound of folding or tearing those
new cardboard cartons was worse than fingernails on the blackboard. But it is weird without it.

We've already paced around the cement slab where the new
house will be, and looked at how the view will be from all the
rooms. They're finally making real progress. The plans are in and
Dad's made a little balsa wood model of what it will look like. With
balsa wood beds and tables and a bath and toilet. There will actually
be a whole bedroom for me, that's at the end of the hallway instead
of opening right onto the kitchen, and while I'm away the boys will
have one each. Everyone's got ideas on what colours things should
be, whether to have paint or wallpaper and what to have on the
floors. Mum and Dad both liked the floor he made in the old house,
but she's sick of polishing it. She just wants tiles and carpet. And a
proper bathroom.

No one wants to think about packing up to move. I don't even
want to think about moving.

This house can look pretty nice when everything's all clean and
polished. That's what I've been doing while Mum and Dad are away
on their holiday. They're only going up to Noosa for a week, but it's
a chance for Dad to give the new VW a run and I'm doing a room
every day as a surprise for Mum when they get back. Sort of a
spring clean I suppose, because it is September.

Thinking about meals is the hardest thing. I mean, we all like bacon and eggs and sausages and fish fingers and chips and things

that are easy to cook, but you can't have them all the time. Mum once said it's always the first thing she thinks about when she wakes up. What to cook for tea. I used to think that was weird. I'm beginning to wonder if being in charge of a family is such fun. Just about once a day there's some major fight happening. Usually at night when I'm just settling in to a good book or whatever I've been looking forward to on TV is about to start.

'Tell him to stop, Cathy.' Tom's voice issues from the darkness beyond the living room, where they were supposedly asleep.

'Stop it Nicky. Don't tease him.'

'Tom's a spaz. Tom's a spaz.'

'Just ignore him.'

'Just ignore 'im. Norim,' now Nicky's giggling and I'm trying not to laugh.

'Shut up, creep features.'

'Pimple face, pimple face, 'Norim, norim.'

'Nicky, be quiet – go to sleep. I'll tell Mum.'

'Ow! He hit me Cathy. He's punching me. Stop it, pimple face. Get over to your side of the room. He hit me in the kidneys.'

'He started it! He always starts it.'

'Liar.'

'I don't care who started it. Just cut it out!' 1 didn't know I could yell so loud.

'I can't stand this,' Tom's voice is hoarse and croaky now, obviously on the verge of tears. 'I hate him. I hate everyone!' Then more quietly, 'Just you wait till tomorrow.'

'I heard that, Tom. Now stop it, once and for all. He's only little, and you should know better.'

'He's only little, he's only little! That's what everyone says. It's not fair. Everyone always listens to his side of the story – Nicky this, Nicky that!'

'Go and sleep in my room if you want to. I don't know why you can't go one day without having all these stupid fights.'

Which all started because of the television. 'Straight to bed after *Pick a Box* every night,' Mum said, 'ok? You can read for a while, but I don't want any arguments.' And they both looked as if to say, who's going to argue?

Sometimes you have to wonder whether it was all worth it. Getting TV.

'You can't watch the *Twilight Zone*,' I told him, 'it's on too late'.

'That's not fair. You watch it all the time. Nicholas gets to watch everything he likes.'

'*Rocky and Bullwinkle* is about the only thing he watches,' I said, 'and that's on before tea. And I've already done all my homework in the kitchen, and put up with the noise from *Pick a Box* and everyone shouting out the answers in the living room before I start watching.'

'You shout out answers too,' he said. Well, that's true, but I'm just listening, not watching.

'You know what Mum said. It's not fair to me if you try and do stuff you're not allowed to. I'm already trying to keep the house tidy, and do all the cooking and everything. I can't stand it with you two fighting.'

Anyway, Tom gets in his share of television time. I mean, we all like to watch the cricket, but Tom is always glued to the set in cricket season, from the time the Test Match starts till the last ball is bowled. Well, when he's not at school. He always buys the little programme book at the newsagent's, the ABC book where they have pictures and biographies of the players and pages at the back with batting and bowling records. In between are all the pages you fill out as the match that's happening now goes on, so you can remember the scores and compare them with the old records.

It's all a bit like the Accounts Ledger that Dad fills out for the farm – incoming and outgoing – wickets taken, number of runs at the fall of each wicket, little diagrams that show you where all those mad positions are, like deep gully and short leg, silly mid- off and silly mid- on. Tom even fills out the sort of ball it was that got someone out – googlies and yorkers, ones that landed in the block hole. He probably doesn't need to fill it all in, he remembers it anyway. He'll probably be able to in twenty years' time. Which is also like Dad. He wants to be an ABC cricket commentator when he grows up. Tom, not Dad. Dad would like to be a pilot when he grows up. But he's got a family now, and the war's over, and Mum doesn't even like flying.

But she loves holidays. And it would be a long time since they've had a chance to do that without kids. In fact they loved it all so much, they must have forgotten what it's really like *with* the kids. They're talking about doing it again next year, maybe as far up as the Barrier Reef, except this time with all of us.

Queensland Coast, September Holidays 1966

CATHY

WE'RE ALL SQUASHED into the VW. Mum and Dad in the front and Tom, Nicky and me in the back seat, as well as bits of luggage that wouldn't fit in the boot. I don't know what we'd do if Susan was still here. Tom's wearing his snorkel and mask that he got last Christmas and hoping we'll see some actual brain coral and tropical fish, instead of just the kelp and barnacles in the tidal pools at South Beach. He says if he's wearing the mask it'll save space in the boot and also he can't see sideways at the stupid faces Nicky's pulling at him. But Nicky's too busy complaining that everyone's sitting on top of him to pull faces at anyone.

Just as well we're not a fat family. Maybe Dad wouldn't have bought a VW if we were, but I don't think the size of us would have made any difference. It's a good car. You get about the best mileage per gallon of anything else around. He's also the sort of person who doesn't like stopping once we get going.

We took a photo at the old car yard where the pink Holden hangs out off the verandah, but we didn't buy any fresh strawberries because they were on the other side of the road, and we had lunch at the Oak Dairy in the hinterland because everyone was dying by then. They make the most delicious, creamy milkshakes you ever tasted. Tom wore his snorkel mask into the cafe too, which was a bit embarrassing, but most other people seemed to think it was funny. Mum made him take it off when he was having his milkshake and he had these red lines around his eyes that made him look like a creature that should have antennas.

Going through the Glass House Mountains was beautiful. When I get a license myself and I'm driving in a car with a bit more room, or if someone who doesn't mind stopping a bit more often is driving, I'll have a proper look round there. Even though the milkshake we had for lunch was lovely, every place we've passed since then had Devonshire Teas on the blackboard, and each one seemed to have a prettier spring garden, or a better view than the last. The lookouts we have stopped at seemed to be a long way from any tearooms.

I'm sure the Barrier Reef – well, Green Island to be precise – will be beautiful when we get there, but sticking to plastic seats and fighting about who gets to sit near the window all the way is not beautiful. And Nicky got car sick, which was definitely not beautiful. When he got back in the car Tom said 'Serves you right, toad face!' because Nicky had been laughing at him and calling him Mr. Spaceman ever since we left the Oak Dairy. Then Mum and Dad both got cranky and told us all to be quiet and not say another word till we got out of the car or we'd be left behind.

God – I mean some people of my age call themselves adults.

TOM

TALK ABOUT A waste of time. He'd said he didn't want to go.

He and Steven had both got selected in the squad for the schools' pre-season twelve and under cricket tryout. Steven's Mum said he could have stayed at their place, but of course his father said 'No, the holiday's already booked and we can't get a refund at this late date.' All right, stiff cheese, but he couldn't see that that was a good enough reason. He didn't book it.

'You can play cricket anytime,' Dad said. 'Of course you'll get into the team. This might be the only chance you ever have to see such a unique piece of the country. Be thankful. Some families couldn't afford it at all.'

Yeah. Well he couldn't get into the team if he wasn't there could he. And he'd better not miss out or they'll all be sorry. It wasn't as if there was acres of spare room in the car either. The only bright spot was that at least he'd finally be able to try his snorkel out on some proper marine life, and see if Mum's new Instamatic worked. Well, maybe not underwater, but the brochures said they had glass-bottomed boats.

Nicholas was the one they should have left at home. What a whinger. And then, just to make the car pong, as well as being like an oven, he was sick everywhere. Cathy said at the Oak Dairy, 'Eergh – I don't know how anyone can stand lime milkshakes.' Little did she know. She must have conveniently forgotten about the whales. Apparently somebody has to throw up every time this family visits an important piece of Australian nature study.

They didn't go through Tangalooma this time, but none of the Whaling Stations are still working now. He was only little, but he'll never forget that trip. That mountain of rubbery red meat that you

196

couldn't believe was just part of one whale. The noise of all those screaming ladies and a million seagulls clacking and fighting over awful grey guts and intestine looking things. And ten million flies. And of course everyone ended up mad at him again. 'How many times do you have to be told?' Dad said, and even Mum didn't talk to him for a while; 'You were told not to lean out over that wall!' But it was only because there were so many flies that he knocked the camera out of the man's hands next to him. One of the men on the flensing floor in those bloody aprons got it back, but it had fallen into a big pile of blubber, and they handed it up to Dad because they thought it was his. Then Cathy had to run away so she wouldn't spew all over everyone. Not that it would have made a lot of difference to the smell if she'd stayed there. It would have fitted right in.

But at least the whales were a sight worth seeing, even if they were dead. He never got to see North Queensland at all. Didn't even get as far as the Tropic of Capricorn. He'd wanted to see whether that was a line across the road, or just a sign saying 'You have reached the Tropic of Capricorn' and you had to take their word for it, or what. In the end it wasn't even a holiday. They didn't see any great natural wonders and they didn't get a refund either.

It was only because of him that something to remember happened on what had to be the most boring trip in the history of the universe. And he'd get a few laughs when the time came for reading out the What Did You Do in the Holidays Composition.

CATHY

THE CAR BROKE down. The closest place they could tow us to was Gympie.

The three of us got to ride in the back of the tow truck on the way there. There's not a lot of scenery on the Glass Highway, and not much after that, at least on the way to Gympie – other than the odd group of black and white cows all standing around and facing in the same direction, or scrubby bush. But back there we got a better look at it, with the sun on our faces and the wind in our hair.

Tom sniffed the air and glared at Nicky over his shoulder, 'Phew, that's better.' Nicky stuck out his tongue and made circles round his eyes. 'Cut it out, you two,' I said, but they did anyway because they could see Mum looking at them through the back window. She'd already ordered them to sit on opposite sides of the truck or face death.

In fact, getting towed was about the most exciting thing that happened all the time from then on. Well, almost. Dad did stop a lot more on the way home. We toured the Ginger Factory, and this time he picked Scenic Lookouts that at least had Forest Walks nearby, some with tearooms. We even stayed a night at Noosa. We had a lot more time to relax, because by the time the car was fixed, almost a week of our two week holiday had been used up, and there wouldn't be enough time to get to the tropics and back. It was all a sort of consolation prize really, because there had to be some part of the big trip north to enjoy. I never thought I'd just want to get home from a holiday.

The thing is, if you asked me what might be a good place to have to spend five days without a car, Gympie would not be on the list. It also ended up being a pretty good place to make you think twice about of a lot of things you thought you liked before – fish and chips, Chinese meals, reading.

There was only one place to stay, apart from the pub, which Dad said looked like a house of ill repute – Nicky said 'What does repute mean?' – and that was the Star Motel. Actually, it was the Star Motl, according to the letters on the front wall next to the office, and the Sta otel when the neon sign came on. It didn't have television and it didn't have a pool. Dad spent a lot of time at the garage, supposedly offering to help so we might get the car fixed in time to still keep heading north, but I think mainly to get out of having to apologise every five minutes for the fact that we were stuck in Gympie. But then the weekend came and they had to send for some car part from Brisbane.

Mum and I tried to sun bake on the patch of lawn behind our unit so we could get some wear out of our new costumes, but it was so hot we just got sweaty and because the winter had been especially dry there was hardly any grass and a million Bindii. You couldn't exactly lie around inside either, except on our beach towels or the orange chenille bedspreads, because the lounge and the chairs were all vinyl and the floor was lino. Tom and Nicky went exploring but said there wasn't anything to see when you got there.

After three days, we'd finished reading all the books we'd brought with us and were back to the breakfast menu – you never knew, it might change one day – and the sorts of magazines you find in the dentist's waiting room. People had left some old ones behind, with all the crosswords half done, as well as the sorts of paperbacks that fall open at particular pages, and Mrs. Bowman had a little bookcase set up in the Front Office with an invitation to Guests – Please Feel Free to Borrow. When we did, Mum found that most of the words that had already been already filled in were wrong.

We'd also borrowed a Chinese Checkers Board, but some of the blue and yellow marbles were missing, and I'm never going to play another game of Hangman or Noughts and Crosses in my life.

We actually got to the stage where it was a bit embarrassing running into Mrs. Bowman a lot, because she'd been good to us letting us keep the same unit and stay at a weekly or a daily rate depending on how long it was going to take the new car part to come, and even lending us a little griller to cook on because she only did dinners twice a week. Then both dinners sounded like variations on the meat she had left over from the weekend roast, so Mum wanted to go somewhere else.

There was a fish and chip shop. We'd had that on the first night, to ease the annoyance of not getting to Maryborough, which had been that day's destination, and once more after we realized we might be annoyed for a few more days. It was all right, but Gympie's not exactly on the beach. You had to wonder where the fish came from and how long ago. The pub specialized in rissoles, curried sausages and corned beef and cabbage, and it all smelt like spilt beer and cigarette smoke and sounded as though there was a greyhound track in there.

We thought a Chinese meal might be good, which was lucky because that was the other choice. 'Let's make a night of it,' Dad said. 'It's not the end of the world.' Anyway, by the time we knew we'd be there for the weekend, we'd had do a bit of unpacking, so we got dressed up in the clothes we *were* going to wear for meals at the Palms Lodge and went out.

When we walked past the Imperial, we could barely hear the dog races over the din of men's voices. It was Friday night. A few other cars had pulled into the Star late in the afternoon and now lights were on in several other rooms beside ours. We knew they'd probably be dark again tomorrow night, but for the evening, most of the passers through seemed to have decided on the same dining venue, and we made quite a jolly crowd in the Red Lion.

The trouble was, initially we thought, 'Poor girl, it is pretty crowded – maybe they're just not used to catering for so many,' or 'Maybe she's new,' but after a while, although the noise from the kitchen meant there had to be a lot of staff out there, we calculated that it must have been longer than three quarters of an hour since the lone waitress had hurried off with our order for a number 12 with pork, a number 14, a 21, a prawn 11, rice fried not steamed, and plates so we could share.

Mum said 'I'm sure that couple with the chocolate sauce and ice cream boy came in after we did.'

'And the Chinese banquet table,' I said, 'I saw them go into the Motl Restaurant when we were leaving.'

'Well, who ordered the prawns,' Dad said, 'they've obviously had to go and catch them.'

'Come on Rob, it isn't funny,' Mum was pulling flailing chopstick daggers away from Tom and Nicky and placing them firmly out of reach, 'I think maybe we should go and see if our order's been forgotten. Got mixed up with some other table or something.'

Tom said 'I'll go, can I go', and I guess Mum was about to say 'Yes', happy to prevent the Soy Sauce War, 'all right, but wait just a minute,' – till the waitress coming up behind you has gone past with that tray – but he put his foot out just at the exact moment and we thought later that it was probably lucky that they weren't our meals. Someone's entrée apparently, so it was mainly spring rolls and dim sims and the soup was clear. A lot of the plates just sort of rolled or bounced on the vinyl tiles.

Mum and Dad apologized like crazy, and made Tom offer to help clean up, but many other Tong family members had suddenly materialized, brows knitted, but smiling, waving mops and towels. 'Not worry, s'allright, only accident.'

When Tom muttered 'Well, that's one way to get attention,' we all had to try not to laugh, because the food wasn't long in coming, but for the rest of the meal we felt several sets of eyes inspecting us through the little glass windows in the swinging doors that led to the kitchen. When our dishes did begin to arrive, two older girls carried out the sweet and sour pork and the beef and black bean sauce. Very slowly and carefully, giving Tom a wide berth. The honey chicken was delivered by Mrs Tong, and the chow mein and fried rice by Mr., whose face registered no emotion either when we asked again about the extra plates, or when we all apologized profusely (again) for causing the accident. Mum kept having to kick us under the table, and say 'There's no point saying you're sorry if you're going to grin like idiots while you're doing it.'

The emptied dishes were removed from our table with a lot more speed than which they'd been brought to it. Our waitress never reappeared. Either she was sitting out the back with her leg up, swelling from a nasty sprain, weeping into her apron with humiliation, or she just refused to come out again while we were still there. Mum suggested at one stage that she might not even be their daughter, and she was there on a try out.

So generally, it got pretty embarrassing for us to go out at all.

You can even get sick of tea and scones.

Never mulberries though. Our tree was weeping with them when we got home.

And as we turned into the driveway, Mum actually said, 'For all its faults, I've never been so happy to see a house in all my life.'

Dad said 'Quick, someone get a pen, write that down: Wednesday – what is it, the twenty first - Wednesday 21st Sept, 1966. Can you repeat that for me, dear?'

She just laughed and said 'Oh get out – I might get you to go and check what those goats have been doing to my new trees up there before I sign anything.'

MARGARET

WELL, THERE ARE degrees. Yes, the house looks beautiful. After Gympie anything would. All anyone coming along the driveway can see is the front corner – rustic, granted, but a comfortable looking farm house of a certain age, the side wall largely hidden by the heavily fruited mulberry tree.

Ignore all the crates, tea chests and bicycles, the tractor, the old ute up on blocks, discarded farm implements that never found their way to the shed – or wouldn't fit, and you look up to the forest green verandah railing with the spring leafed grapevine curling along its length and up the side posts, framing the front windows green panelled door and white walls. You don't see that the back and far side walls are still partly unpainted, that one of the windows on the back verandah sports a tar paper patch, and there are untold horrors inside that will remain that way now; horrors that she can almost ignore now, since the plans for the new house have finally been approved.

She and Rob are even pretty much in agreement on all the details. The fact is, she's been saying for so long 'I'd just be happy with a proper bathroom' that the reality of being able to plan for and make choices about such luxuries as tiles, carpets, kitchen cabinets, a new stove, built in wardrobes, doors – sliding or otherwise, not just a bath but what colour bath, is all quite dizzying.

The move can't come soon enough. And there'll be no tears shed by her. No nostalgia. And those wretched goats better not have escaped. All right, so they'll eat anything, but there seems to be a definite preference for anything new, green and vaguely ornamental. She can see why the devil is often represented with what look like goat's horns. Anyone other than Rob trying to shoo or yell at them is invariably met with that slow deliberate sideways chewing of whatever precious plant they have started on, and a glassy stare from those rectangular-pupiled eyes. Perversely, they will let him hand feed them, come when he calls, and go wherever he bids.

One of the things she's most looking forward to is having the space and reason to create a decent garden. Rob's been able to suggest all sorts of plants and flowers that will really thrive in the climate – though she can't imagine anything not doing so in this red soil. When they first arrived at McClaren's Ridge, he planted a couple of Bunya Pines, as well as silky oaks and flame trees to mark the upper boundary of the new house block, all of which have had time to mature into beautiful trees. There is also a Poinciana, coming along well, which will screen the new house from the road, and provide shade for the rockery, planned to cover the slope down to the door. From what will effectively be the front of the house, as much glass as possible opens onto the panoramic view to the northeast, from the living area, the kitchen and the main bedroom.

And not only is she genuinely pleased to be back, despite the efforts first of the heifers and now of the wild eyed goats, most of her carefully nurtured, frangipanis have survived. For the garden beds, she wants masses of colour and scent, azaleas and gardenias; if they're not supposed to be suited to this area, she'll find a way. Nothing too delicate, and certainly no thorns; she's never been interested in becoming an orchid fancier, a rose breeder. The girls at golf have already promised all sorts of cuttings.

But no, definitely no nostalgia. It's not as if they're actually leaving McClaren's Ridge. To finally have screened windows, and live without the claustrophobia of mosquito nets, hell to wash and constantly in need of patching – *how many times do I have to tell you boys, keep your toenails cut, otherwise, mend your own nets or get bitten; it's up to you* – without the sinus inducing smoke from the ever present summer burning coils, (citronella might smell better, but mozzies seem to think so too), to say goodbye to the outdoor toilet, home to several huntsmen, probably redbacks and carpet snakes as well, that no one wants to go near at night. Even Rob will be glad to move on from that fond memory, since he's always had the unthinkable task of emptying its contents and digging the pit on a regular basis. With remarkable stoicism she might add. What's the point of complaining he's always said, but then he would.

Even despite the gradual added comforts – they actually have a bona fide lounge suite now, fitted sisal matting in the lounge room and bedrooms, the television – all the creaks and groans, the leaks, the dust brought in by the relentless northerlies of October and November, the timber that is no doubt rotting quietly in hidden places, or will one day succumb to the one white ant infestation Rob hasn't beaten at the source, the kitchen in summer: as hot as the slow combustion oven that needs to be kept alight so they have hot water, the southern exposure to the afternoon storms – all these things are the Old House, as is the constant feeling that what nearly happened once could happen again, that the whole place is at the mercy of the elements and could blow off its stumps in the next high wind.

But it won't be long. The builders Rob has settled on are teed up, after much negotiation and long, long agonizing. Thank god he's working away from the farm now, and not only because of the money. If he was going to be around when they started work on the house, they'd have him watching their every move.

And the money has been wonderful, on top of which, Rob being Rob – no job could be done properly as far as he's concerned unless he's read every available journal, article, or piece of research on it – his growing expertise has led him to a position where he has been asked to act as consultant on a third world agricultural project, which means a trip overseas. *It'll probably be a one off, a lump sum. And it's a lot. I really can't afford to knock it back. Why don't you come with me? Part of it falls during the school holidays – the boys would cer-*

tainly enjoy a trip away – I'm sure Susan and Ross wouldn't mind taking them for a couple of weeks. You'd love it.

She knows this is incomprehensible to him, so she's not even bothered trying to voice it, but she can't imagine anything she'd love less than wandering around some place all day while Rob is off from dawn till dusk at seed conferences and farm demonstrations, in a country where she knows no one and doesn't speak the language, fascinating or not. Why can't people just let her stay in one place.

McClaren's Ridge, Christmas 1967

CATHY

I STILL COME home for all the breaks. I slip into my home-for-the-holidays cocoon.

Easter is always chocolate, hot cross buns and more chocolate. Cooler nights coming in. You can stay snuggled into sleep-warmed home feeling blankets till toasting cinnamon bun smells fill the house and it's sunny enough to go out and lie under the clear blue days that will be the last of summer. And no excuse needed because there's always course reading to be done.

A suntan is the main thing. The beach is better, but the back yard's okay. You can actually wear less – I'd never be game to wear Susan's bikinis in public - but the ants fight for their territory. Then there's the rotisserie routine: lay out your towel, find reading matter completely unrelated to study texts, slather yourself in coconut oil and turn every half hour. In other words, get as burnt as you can (without peeling) in four or five days before heading back to early winter at Uni, so everyone is envious that you live on the coast and might even be a surfie.

I'm still in my old bed with the drawers underneath, and the schoolbooks – all those ruled exercise books filled with neat fountain pen writing that looks like someone else's, headings underlined in red. Carefully coloured drawings of pyramids, wildlife of the Amazon, products of the Ruhr Valley, compositions with red ticks, pages of trigonometry with "could do better". I still fall asleep to the distant boom of breaking waves, wake to the bird-calls of McClaren's Ridge, and breathe in the green and the salt and the red clay soil.

The dusty chains of campus life, with nothing but distant hills and more hazy land on the horizon, fall away. The world outside is like a coat you take off at the start of the gravel road.

But there were changes that Christmas.

In town I stepped off the Greyhound into a glassy, modernised bus terminal and across the road where the Norfolk pines had lined the banks of South Beach estuary, bulldozers were busy levelling reclaimed land for more houses, a shopping centre, and a new hospital. I saw Leanne Thompson across the road, but I don't think she saw me, and I didn't wave when we drove past. I suddenly thought about Christine, coming back for holidays after she went to the school in Brisbane. I could probably talk to her now; tell her I know how it feels. But it's been too long. We don't even write letters anymore.

The road home was bitumen nearly all the way to McClaren's Ridge – which didn't seem that far out of town anymore.

Lovetts' road hadn't changed; still unsealed and only wide enough for one car, but instead of turning off into the first hard-packed dirt driveway up the hill after Lovetts', we drove straight past our old house, turned sharply at the top of the hill, bumped over a piece of concrete guttering and coasted down a new paved driveway into a new carport.

White bricks, painted roof, sliding glass doors. Everything about the new house made what you could still see of the old one through the trees look rustier. Sad and lopsided. There were plans for the new share farmer to move in but it was still empty. Harry looked after Robinsons' dairy farm full time now, because Wal was getting on.

'The ship's come in then?' I said. Dad sort of grinned and shrugged, and Mum said 'Well, the rowing boat maybe.'

We were moving in. Well, up - higher up the ridge actually.

The new house looked down on the jacarandas and mango trees instead of being sheltered by them, the way we used to be. But a healthy row of frangipanis lined the edge of the lawn that looked towards the sea and the young garden already featured a feathery, spreading Poinciana, because Mum's vigilance had outlasted the persistence of hungry wandering heifers. And the experiment with angora goats.

Tasks were assigned. While Mum found places in cupboards for things that had never had proper places before, Dad set about rectifying various messes he'd known the builders would make. Tom and Nicky alternated between fighting over who would have my room when I wasn't there and flushing the new toilet, and I installed myself on the new-carpet smelling floor, cardboard cartons and wooden crates stacked and overflowing around me, and set about Organising-the-Books. Sixteen years' worth of books. Not to mention what came up from Melbourne before that. Arranging them on the new shelves that were one complete wall of the new living room.

Groups of Shakespeares were set together. Comedies and tragedies in paperback and hard covered Complete Editions, as well as all the Faulkners, all the orange and white Penguins and all the *Reader's Digest Book Club* selections. *Arthur Mee's Children's Encyclopedias* – all ten volumes including Index – were lined up together near The *Shorter Oxford* and others, as well as a Funk & Wagnall that someone had to buy because they couldn't be rude to the salesman. *The Decameron* rubbed shoulders with *The Reader's Bible* because the covers went well together and they were the same size. The *Naughtiest Girl in School* sat next to Walter Scott, the Romantic Poets were stacked up beside John O'Hara and Ernest Hemingway, *East of Eden*, *Fishing the East Coast*, *Gone with the Wind*, *Wind in the Willows*, *The*

Water Babies, Dr Spock's Baby and Child Care – and on. With occasional stops to wallow in feeling tragic by rereading bits like The Piper at the Gates of Dawn, Byron's *So We'll go no More A'Roving*, the last pages of *The Great Gatsby*. Till the boxes were empty and the glass doors polished, finger marks newspapered clean with metho. One of the top shelves for trophies, certificates and studio photos that none of us looked like anymore. It looked lovely by the end of the holidays.

And probably saved me from feeling as though I was staying in a hotel. A bedroom all to myself, with a door that closed if I wanted it to. I didn't – it already felt like my room at college – on loan. But the furnishings were my familiars and I could still see the Southern Cross from the window at night. And there was still hot Christmas dinner on a hot Christmas day.

The End of Summer 1969

CATHY

I DIDN'T GO home for Easter in 1968. It was really close to the end of term anyway, and an excursion to the Blue Mountains – well, actually, someone in the group who was going to the Blue Mountains – was enough to tempt me away from the ocean. I called in to Vaucluse too, when I came down from Katoomba, to see Aunty Jean and Uncle Harold. The house felt empty; everything perfect and not a hair out of place, but very empty.

The photo that was taken of Melvin at the Bird Century was on the mantelpiece. 'He loved that holiday,' said Aunty Jean, 'Didn't he, Harold?' Uncle Harold made a sort of impatient, throat-clearing noise and retreated behind his *Financial Times*. They hadn't had a letter either. 'He'll be all right,' I said, 'as long as he's wearing his hat and his mosquito lotion.'

And I hope there are lots of birds there too, wherever he is.

When I did go home, in May, Mrs. Robinson had died.

Mrs. Robinson, who'd never seemed to have a sick day in her life. She looked after everyone else. I had left home when they discovered that she had cancer; had probably had it so long that it was too late to do anything. 'I think she'd known for a long time,' Mum said, 'I always thought it was more than just Hilda leaving.'

'Hilda?' Dad said.

'*Blue Hills*,' said Mum, 'Hilda – the cook.' Except for things like births or bushfires, Mrs. Robinson had never missed an episode of *Blue Hills*. Then when Hilda –at least, the actress who read the part –

211

fell ill and had to be written out of the show, it was as though Mrs. Robinson had lost a personal friend. There were days when she didn't even bother to tune in.

We drove past the cemetery on the way to McClaren's Ridge. 'So Mrs. Robinson is home at last', Mum said.

'And Wal wants to be,' said Dad. The Robinsons had adjoining plots organized a long time ago. In the Scottish corner. Whenever Mrs. Robinson had talked about going home, she usually meant going home to God, or Scotland.

And her funeral, or what lead up to it, had been the stuff of drama, but real-life drama, too terrible even for a *Blue Hills* episode.

There would have been no sun baking that Easter. It had rained for the whole four days as it sometimes does in April. Thunderous, beating on the tin roof rain. Storms that would turn cattle tracks on the hillsides into gushing trenches, summerfulls of rotting leaves sluicing from overflowing gutters into frog-croaking drainpipes, and gumboot footprints criss-crossing back verandahs.

And that's when Mrs. Robinson had given up the fight, Mum said. As though she couldn't find the energy to cope with the prospect of one more flood or cyclone. Harry Robinson came over in the wet dark, late on Easter Saturday, to tell Mum and Dad that he didn't think his mother would see out the night. His father wasn't really taking it in, he'd said.

She died just before dawn on the Sunday.

That same afternoon, Harry and Mr. Robinson had both come to our back door, knocking frantically to be heard above the rain.Distraught. Harry had been trying to make arrangements with the undertakers since early morning, but he'd had trouble getting anyone from the Funeral Home to come. 'Mum had it all organized,' he said. She'd wanted a nice funeral of course, but no fuss. 'Just telephone Mr. Parker when the time comes, love' she'd said to him, 'they'll know what to do.'

But they hadn't been that keen to come out. They would do their best in this time of tragedy, but old Mr. Parker wasn't that well himself and Ralph was away. Easter was always a difficult time, the weather looked like it was really set in, and what with McClaren's Ridge being so far out … . Eventually, Ivan – the youngest of the Parkers – Undertakers You Can Rely On (to be parked forever, people said), had arrived, though how on earth had they thought just one of them would be able to manage … and now he was in trouble. They'd got Mrs. Robinson into the back, but Ivan had taken the turn out from Robinson's gate too fast and skidded. Got bogged, just like everyone had warned him he would if he didn't take it slow and easy. Now he wasn't game to brake or accelerate too hard, and every time he moved he was just seesawing in and out of the wheel ruts that acted like tramlines up and down Robinson's hill.

Dad went out into the pouring rain with them to help, but it was getting late and cold and dangerous. Exhaust fumes billowed through the grey, sheeting rain and the big heavy car was rocking and sliding and getting closer to the verge every time they tried to pull him back onto the track with ropes and chocks. Suddenly he did get loose and the tyres spun and red mud flew up and plastered the men's streaming faces and the hearse lurched over the edge of the road and ended up with its nose pointed down towards Robinson's gully and the milking shed.

It was dreadful, Dad said. They had to leave it all as it was and they'd had to leave it overnight because it was dark by then and nothing could be done. He also said that by the time Ivan Parker got back up to the road he'd finally looked as if getting his good black suit and his black shoes and shiny car muddy wasn't the worst that could happen.

But the most terrible part was Wal. Dad said he'd never forget how he looked out there then – like you'd imagine King Lear, white haired, wild and weeping in the storm. He'd lost his life's centre.

It was strange for all of us, without Mrs. Robinson. Even though I hadn't seen a lot of her since I went away, it was sad coming home and knowing that she wasn't there anymore. She was the only one who made us feel like we weren't outsiders when we first moved to McClaren's Ridge, and she was always there for chats and cups of tea – a safe harbour – especially for Mum in those first years, a city girl with two new babies and no electricity.

You just didn't drop in on Wal the way you could with Mrs. Robinson. Harry, the only one not married and still at home, was always neat and tidy, but the house would never smell of fresh scones anymore and the lino would get dull. Wal had never really managed to do much without Mrs. Robinson except grow prize pansies and make all his daughters want to leave McClaren's Ridge. It had sort of surprised him when she got sick. And although he stayed alive, it was not much of a living.

He never looked any different. Ever since we'd known Mr. Robinson, he'd been a tall, fiercely craggy man with bushy eyebrows who stood no nonsense from anyone except Mrs. Robinson, and she was about the only one who wasn't a bit afraid of him. It wasn't hard to believe the story Susan told about him cutting Maisie Simpson off when she married a Lovett. Keeping the old feud alight. But now there was nothing happening in his eyes. And you had to yell, or keep repeating things before he would know what you were saying to him.

He went for long walks around the farm and talked to himself, or just sat in the empty kitchen. Where the hearse had slipped, the grass had grown back, but there were still two deep grooves at the side of the track, and you often saw him at that spot. Standing there, looking out to the ranges on the far side of the valley. The McClaren farm was long gone, but that was where Mrs. Robinson had grown up. Her family had run dairy cows on the other side of the western slopes and Harry thought that sometimes when his father was gone all day he'd probably gone looking for her, following the journey he'd have made many times in their courting days, to confront old Mr. McClaren, who, by all accounts, made even Wal Robinson look good-tempered. But many of the paths he had walked then were lost in the undergrowth. New brick houses stood in places that used to be paddocks. Everything without Iris was confusing,

Harry said his Dad was all right. There wasn't much you could do.

Nicky was eleven by then and, with Tom, the last of us kids still at home. Mr. Robinson didn't recognize him sometimes because he really only remembered him as a new baby, from when Mum took him up to show Mrs. Robinson, or when he was still a toddler and Mr. Robinson had let him feed the poddy calf. After we'd got the Station Wagon we hadn't needed to get lifts into town with the Robinsons so much, and once we got television the boys never went up to visit after school the way Susan and I used to.

One day, at the start of the surf-club season, towards the end of that same year, Nick went up to sell Harry some raffle tickets for the Nippers. Mr. Robinson was home by himself and Nick said he felt as though he shouldn't try to get him to buy any because it wasn't really fair. He said he was trying to picture Mr. Robinson at the beach, in his big bush hat, dusty boots and braces, and suddenly thought maybe he couldn't even swim. Anyway, he did ask him, since he was there and there were only a few more tickets left in the book. Mr. Robinson said 'What's the price?' and Nick said 'They're ten cents or three for twenty cents.'

Decimal currency was all a bit of a mystery to Wal. *Just another one of those stupid foreign ideas.* It all happened round about the time Mrs. Robinson started to get really ill and he still talked in zacs and pennies and quids. He repeated, 'What's the price?' and Nick told him again but he still didn't seem to understand. 'What's the price?' He kept asking and Nick got a bit impatient and said again, very slowly, but very loudly 'Ten cents, or three for twenty!' And finally, Mr. Robinson got a bit fiery – those faded blue eyes actually looked at him, Nick said – a lot like the old Wal.

'Righto sonny,' he said then, 'keep your hair on,' and he stumped over to the kitchen dresser. 'Give us a couple,' he said, and pushed a handful of coins at Nick. Exactly the right money for six tickets, which was just as many as Nick had left. 'Gosh, thanks, Mr. Robinson,' Nick said, but Wal looked as if he'd forgotten about raffle tickets already and Nick was glad to escape.

And then, just before he went to sleep, Nicky was remembering the conversation, and he suddenly realized that what Wal had been saying was 'What's the prize?'

He wanted to run back to Robinson's right then and apologize for being so awful and not understanding, but it was far too late to do that, and tomorrow was a school day. He promised himself that he'd go up after school and tell Wal what the raffle prize was.

But the next day one of our heifers got out. Dad went down to bring it back, and found Wal lying face down in the paddock above Robinson's dam. Before Nick could tell him it was a television.

'A portable television, Mr. Robinson. You could have one in your own room. And beach towels, for second prize. Two big striped ones, with a fringe and a matching beach umbrella.'

Wal didn't need to check the water pump anymore. It was a steep walk and Harry always did it anyway. He'd probably had one or two minor strokes already the doctor said, but this one was massive. Dad said he looked as though he'd simply fallen where he stood, more surprised than in pain. He also said he wouldn't mind if that was the way it happened to him when the time came and Mum said for heavens sake Rob. I knew what he meant, but sometimes it makes me cry when I think of it.

I was away when Wal died too.

Each time I go back, things are just a bit different.

Mc Claren's Ridge/Sydney, October 1970

MARGARET

THE GARDEN IS beautiful at this time of year; begonias flowering, bright daubs of colour amongst the foliage, the jacarandas sweeping gracefully under the weight of their lavender-blue crinolines; pee-wees, magpies, butcher birds, wrens and swallows, all nesting, all vying for attention with the loudest and most musical song, many almost tame. She never tires of watching the kookaburras from the kitchen window, beaks clamped on the offcuts of raw meat she sometimes leaves out for them, as they play out their own small parody of beating a still writhing snake into submission on the verandah railing. She cuts the first of the season's gardenias, two pure white and still beaded with early morning dew, two more like tiny half-furled cream and white parasols – they will open in the vase, and carries them inside just in time to catch the phone before it stops ringing. It'll be Rob, she hopes.

He's away again. The job's paying good money at last, he's made it his own – become such an expert on pasture improvement that he's always being asked to help set up agricultural development programmes in countries where they need to be developed – which usually means trips to godforsaken places like Uganda, or Colombia or wherever else a crazy dictator is installed or a war is happening, or both. 'Why don't you go and see the family in Sydney? Better still, come with me,' he'll say, but she can't stand flying. And the thought of floating in a tin trap all that distance over sea, to a place where she doesn't know the language and would be alone most of the time while Rob works, is not something she wants to contemplate. Trains are all right, but really, she'd rather stay here – plenty to do in the garden, golf game improving every week, and anyway, she can't leave the boys.

It is Rob, calling from some airport in Rome, which is, incredibly, a stopover on his return flight from Africa – the only available connection. Even he hates this part. Sometimes what amounts to almost two days spent in transit lounges and in cramped seats on a plane, and never quite enough time in interesting cities to do any worthwhile exploring. However, it is the news she wanted to hear. He sounds more than ready to be on his way home, and will phone again when he arrives in Sydney.

Taking care not to bruise the petals, she arranges the gardenias in her favourite vase, a beautiful glazed bowl he brought back from one or other of his travels. Their heady scent is already pervading the airy, light-filled house – the new house. She can't help smiling to herself. She can almost admit that this is it, finally: carpet on the floor, no more floor boards to polish, paved concrete car port – red mud staying outside where it belongs, electric stove, hot water at the turn of a tap, television, semi-automatic washing machine. No need to worry about dinner tonight – Rob won't be back till late tomorrow night, Tom's got cricket practice after school so she'll pick up fish and chips for herself and the boys when she goes to collect him. She's just about to go and have a wallow in the bath when the phone rings again.

Long distance, it's Tess, her youngest sister. Ma's sick again, in hospital this time, and maybe not coming out. This is not unexpected, but her initial feeling is one of panic. How can arrangements be made with Rob away? She doesn't want to have to fly, sleepers often need to be booked months in advance – 'Of course you can – wait till Rob phones and let us know if you like. Or I can make bookings from this end,' – and, she is suddenly aware that Tess, who must already be bearing the responsibility organizing everything in Sydney, is assuming the role of comforter and organizer for her.

'No,' she says, 'sorry, it's just the shock I guess. I'll make some phone calls; let you know as soon as I can. Can I talk to Ma? Are you at home now or the hospital …'

It's only after Tess has given her more detail about their mother's condition, what the doctors have said, who else she has contacted, who'll be staying where, that she starts to think ahead to the journey, to what is shaping up to be a family reunion of sorts, but will probably also be a wake. It's ages since she's seen some of the boys, not seen some of the nieces and nephews since they were toddlers. A couple of times each year, someone from hers or Rob's family has usually made it north for a holiday in the sun, so except for Susan's wedding, going back to the city has not seemed necessary. She telephones the Railway Station, a decision, a physical act of any sort, suddenly necessary to fight off the heaviness, the web of grey inertia that threatens to eclipse the spring morning.

They're all there to meet her at Central. The boys sombre, Tess teary. So familiar yet strangers really, as adults. Stiff hugs at first, then she relaxes into the warmth – that physical ease with siblings that has never been part of her other friendships. And the instinctive feeling that she is back home and will be looked after, followed by the cold realization that the core of this home, the reason they are all here, is crumbling and will soon be gone. Their mother has been given morphine for the pain and is drifting in and out of consciousness. They are going straight to the hospital.

Everyone is worried that Carmel might not be able to make a connecting flight from America in time. By the time she does arrive, a day later, their mother has slipped into a coma from which she does not recover and Carmel is distraught. Margaret still feels as though she is walking through a fog. What does 'being there on time' mean, after all? When she arrived, Ma was still conscious for periods, but heavily sedated. She's not sure her mother even knew who she was.

In the days that follow, she succumbs to the merry-go-round of visitors, well-meaning neighbours and acquaintances, barely remembered from her own childhood. Cups of tea, polite exchanges in which no one actually mentions the word death, but everyone is terribly sympathetic, and apparently interested in knowing what little Meg has been doing all these years up there in the tropics. *You're such a stranger these days.* Such details keep them talking without having to discuss the impending funeral, and life after mother. *You're looking well – well, under the circumstances – country life must be agreeing –lovely to see you, what a pity it has to be such a sad occasion - such a long time since we've seen you – you'll have noticed some changes down here I'd say …*

She's amazed, in fact, by how much the same it all is. She's the one who's changed. She is a visitor, an observer of the preparations, the ritual of the funeral, the social gatherings before and after, the endless obligatory small talk. She's going to have to try to give up smoking all over again when she leaves.

She'd been dreading the funeral. She can never read about or watch depictions of the supposedly typical Irish Catholic family wake as a sort of festive, drunken, joyous occasion, without having to close her eyes against the terror she felt as a small child. Her vain recoil from being made to file past an open coffin and be lifted up by her father to kiss her grandmother's dead cheek. She'd vowed that when she grew up she'd never put her own children through such an ordeal; that she would stay as far away from funerals as possible. With the result that since they'd left the city, she had managed exactly that. The same went for churches, to the point where she'd been worried that she'd make a fool of herself by having obviously forgotten all the hymns and responses. But the Nuns had done their job well; after a few minutes she'd not even needed to follow the elaborately printed Liturgy. She was a wind-up toy and the key was turned – everything still imprinted on a long unused corner of her brain.

She envies Tess her ability to play hostess to all these people – mostly lifelong acquaintances, granted, but still. In a shock of recognition, she remembers that while there are many times she has felt the pull of family very strongly, and she was definitely facing the unknown when she'd headed north with Rob all those years ago, one of the reasons she'd not been unhappy to follow was her increasing sense of claustrophobia, the lack of privacy that came with being part of a big family. She had wanted to escape.

And now there's all this hurrying – the constant feeling that there's no time to sit down and relax, just be still. There's always somewhere else to be, and it's already time you were leaving. She has memories of living and working here, walking down George Street, shopping, catching the suburban train, city circle, going to the pictures, picnics at Bondi, adapted to a pace she did not see as frenetic. Probably it wasn't, twenty five, thirty years ago. Perhaps then it was fun, challenging. She was single then. Only this morning she was just about to sit down to a cup of tea when Tess came rushing in: no time, don't want to miss the train. She can see that this is only Tess's way of coping – of carrying on – things to do, people to see – she can't let herself think about Ma till it's all over; the church, the wake, the food, the house full, then finally empty of guests. Margaret's tried to help, but her own sadness makes her offers sound by turns, abrupt or apathetic.

After a few days, it does get easier, just a matter of making sure you've got half an hour up your sleeve all the time. But knowing that she will be away from it all by the end of the week is all that keeps her going.

She is sleeping in what has always been her mother's bedroom, sharing the double bed with Carmel in a bizarre return to the essence of a childhood spent in this same house. As in the church, she is on the same stage, but here there is no rote script to rely on. She misses the boys, she wishes Rob was here, but she knows his presence would be superfluous. She feels suffocated a lot of the time, by the continuous tumble of people, by the sympathy, the sadness, and the pain. She needs to grieve in private. Most days are so full of family doings that there's little time to think, but when she does allow herself that luxury, she finds herself thinking of McClaren's Ridge.

Car 4, Seat 36 – a berth all to herself. She'll be back in Booralla by tomorrow afternoon. Tess, Mick and their kids are waiting to wave her off, everyone promising that it won't be so long this time between visits. The Guard looks in to see that she is settled and will be comfortable. He will be back to make up the bed at Gosford. During the refreshment stop. For now, yes, she is comfortable.

She stows all the Sydney parcels on the luggage shelf above the seat, unwraps the new John O'Hara she bought on the Station and suddenly remembers Evelyn Timmins and *The Grapes of Wrath*. Lunch in the Railway Restaurant, what was it – sixteen years ago.

She remembers standing on the Headland at Shell Bay, after the cyclone, terrified of a future that had no shape. Desperate to the point where she could clearly imagine rushing down to jump on the train that was taking Mrs. Timmins back to her family, away from the farm. She's forgotten where she put that old railway timetable, but it is still at home somewhere. Cathy came across it when she was sorting out the books in the new house. She doesn't need it now. She read and reread it so often in those early days the pages became soft and dog-eared. She memorized it and played it in her head like the anagrams and word games she used in crosswords. Like song lyrics and poetry, she'd known it off by heart.

She leans back in the seat, gazing at the diminishing skyline as the train gathers speed, north out of Strathfield. Mrs. Timmins was returning to the city. Margaret is going home.

Acknowledgments

For advice and professional guidance on the development of this manuscript, thanks to various tutors from the James Cook University Creative Writing Course, to the Northern Rivers Writers' Centre, (in particular, the mentorship of Marele Day), and to Peter Bishop from Varuna.

Thanks to past and present members of my Writing Group, to my partner Eric and to my family for readings, review, support and feedback, especially to Chris for his help with design and production.

And thank you finally, to Mum and Dad, whose spirits inhabit these pages.

Betsy Roberts has spent most of her life on the Far North Coast of New South Wales. She has had stories published in *Vacations & Travel* magazine, *The Australian Women's Weekly,* and the Prana Writers' Gold Coast Anthology, *Undertow. Summer Feet* is her first novel.